"I won't! My father will give you enough to buy this dirty little fishing boat ten times over"—Harvey stamped on the deck—"if you take me to New York safe.

On top of all that, you want me to do maid's work till the fall? I tell you I will not. Understand?"

Disko Troop looked up at the main mast of his ship with deep interest for a while, as Harvey hollered fiercely all around him.

"Hush!" he said at last. "I'm fig-urin' out my responsibilities in my own mind. It's a matter o' judgment." . . .

"No!" said Harvey. "Take me back to New York or I'll—"

He did not exactly remember what followed. He was lying in the gutter of the ship, holding on to a bloody nose while Troop looked down on him calmly.

A Background Note about
Captains Courageous

Captains Courageous takes place in the mid-1800s. At this time, boats were a common way to travel. Harvey Cheyne is traveling to Europe on a "steamer," which is a passenger ship with a steam-powered engine. He is rescued by a "schooner," a large sailboat typically used for long fishing expeditions. A schooner has at least two masts, and numerous sails that are raised and lowered in order to propel the ship.

Most of the novel takes place on the Grand Banks. This is a shallow area of the North Atlantic Ocean, just southeast of Newfoundland. It is still known today as one of the richest fishing grounds in the world. In the mid-1800s, many men made their living by fishing the Grand Banks. It was an extremely dangerous job that would keep them at sea for months. Like the characters in *Captains Courageous*, most of these men lived in the small coastal towns of New England such as Gloucester, Massachusetts.

Because of his wealth, Harvey is considered "upper class" by society. Although they are not poor, the fishermen would still be thought of as "lower class" because they do not have a formal education. In the everday world, Harvey would have never interacted with the men who ultimately save his life.

Captains
COURAGEOUS

RUDYARD
KIPLING

Edited, and with an Afterword,
by Peggy Kern

 THE TOWNSEND LIBRARY

CAPTAINS COURAGEOUS
A Story of the Grand Banks

TP THE TOWNSEND LIBRARY

For more titles in the Townsend Library,
visit our website: **www.townsendpress.com**

All new material in this edition is
copyright © 2007 by Townsend Press.
Printed in the United States of America

0 9 8 7 6 5 4 3 2

ISBN 13: 978-1-59194-084-5
ISBN 10: 1-59194-084-2

Library of Congress Control Number:
2006935721

CONTENTS

CHAPTER 1

I plowed the land with horses,
But my heart was ill at ease,
For the old sea-faring men
Came to me now and then,
With their sagas of the seas.
—*Longfellow*

The storm door of the smoking room had been left open to the North Atlantic fog, as the big passenger ship rolled and lifted, whistling to warn the fishing fleet.

"That Cheyne boy's the biggest nuisance aboard," said a man in a wool overcoat, shutting the door with a bang. "He isn't wanted here. He's a brat."

A white-haired German reached for a sandwich, and grunted between bites: "I know der breed. America is full of dot kind."

"Oh, stop complaining. There's no real harm to him. He's more to be pitied than anything,"

1

said a man from New York, as he lay along the cushions under the wet skylight. "They've dragged him around from hotel to hotel ever since he was a kid. I was talking to his mother this morning. She's a lovely lady, but she don't pretend to have much control over him. He's going to Europe to finish his education."

"Education hasn't begun yet." This was said by a man from Philadelphia, who was curled up in a corner. "That boy gets two hundred dollars a month in allowance, he told me. He ain't sixteen yet, either."

"Railroads, his father, ain't it?" said the German.

"Yep. That and mines and lumber and shipping. Built one place at San Diego, the old man has; another at Los Angeles; owns half a dozen railroads, half the lumber on the Pacific, and lets his wife spend the money," said the man from Philadelphia in a lazy voice. "She doesn't like California, she says. She just travels around with the boy, trying to find out what'll keep him happy, I guess. Florida, the Adirondacks, New York, and 'round again. All that moving can't be good for him. When he's finished in Europe, he'll be a real troublemaker."

"Why can't the father take care of him personally?" said the voice from the wool coat.

"The old man's too busy. Don't want to be disturbed, I guess. He'll find out his mistake in a few years. Too bad, because there's a heap of good in the boy if you could get at it."

Once more the door banged, and a thin, small boy about fifteen years old, a half-smoked cigarette hanging from one corner of his mouth, leaned into the room. It was clear that he was trying very hard to act older than his age. He was dressed in expensive clothes: a cherry-colored blazer, short pants, red stockings, and bicycle shoes, with a red cap on the back of his head. His pale complexion did not look healthy on a boy his age, who should be tan and weathered from playing outdoors. After whistling between his teeth, as he looked over the company, he said in a loud, high voice: "Say, it's thick with fog outside. You can hear the fishing boats squawking all around us. Say, wouldn't it be great if we ran one over?"

"Shut the door, Harvey," said the New Yorker. "Shut the door and stay outside. You're not wanted here."

"Who'll stop me?" he answered. "Did you pay for my ticket, Mister Martin? 'Guess I've as much right as the next man."

He picked up some dice from a checkerboard and began tossing them from one hand to the other.

"Say, gen'elmen, this is boring. Can't we play a game of poker between us?"

There was no answer, and he puffed his cigarette and drummed on the table with rather dirty fingers. Then he pulled out a roll of bills as if to count it.

"How's your mamma this afternoon?" a man said. "I didn't see her at lunch."

"In her private room, I guess. She's always sick on the ocean. I'm going to give the stewardess fifteen dollars for taking care of her. I don't go down more 'n I can avoid. It makes me feel nervous to walk around down there. Say, this is the first time I've been on the ocean."

"Oh, don't apologize, Harvey."

"Who's apologizing? This is the first time I've crossed the ocean, gen'elmen, and, except the first day, I haven't been sick one little bit. No, sir!" He brought down his fist with a triumphant bang, licked his finger, and went on counting the bills.

"Oh, you're a high-grade machine" the Philadelphian yawned. "You'll blossom into a credit to your country if you're not careful."

"I know it. I'm an American—first, last, and all the time. I'll show 'em that when I hit Europe. Hah! My cigarette's out. I can't smoke that rubbish the ship attendant sells. Any gen'el-man got a real Turkish cigar on him?"

The chief engineer entered for a moment, red, smiling, and wet.

"Say, Mac," cried Harvey cheerfully, "how are we hitting it?"

"Very much in the ordinary way," was his unsmiling reply.

A low chuckle came from a corner. The German opened his cigar case and handed a skinny black cigar to Harvey.

"Dot is the proper cigar to smoke, my young friend," he said. "You vill try it? Yes? Den you vill be ever so happy."

Harvey lit the ugly thing with a dramatic wave of his hand. He felt that he was doing very well in grownup society.

"It would take more 'n this to knock me over," he said, unaware that he was lighting a terrible cigar—a Wheeling "stogie."

"Dot we shall presently see," said the German. "Where are we now, Mr. Mactonal?"

"We'll be on the Grand Bank tonight," said the engineer. "But in a general way o' speakin', we're all among the fishing boats now. We've come close to hitting three of them since noon. Now that's close sailing, ye might say."

"You like my cigar, eh?" the German asked, for Harvey's eyes were full of tears.

"Fine, full flavor," he answered through shut teeth. "Guess we've slowed down a little, haven't we? I'll skip out and see."

"I might if I vhas you," said the German.

Harvey staggered over the wet decks to the nearest rail. He was feeling quite sick, but then he saw the deck attendant and since he had bragged in front of the man that he was never seasick, his pride made him go to the second deck at the back of the ship. The deck was deserted, and he crawled to the very end of it. There he doubled over in helpless agony, for the Wheeling "stogie" and the shaking of the ship's propellers made him feel very ill. His head swelled; sparks of fire danced before his eyes; his body seemed to lose weight, while his legs felt weak in the breeze. He was fainting from seasickness, and a roll of the ship tilted him over the railing onto the outer ledge of the deck. Then a low, gray wave swept out of the fog and pulled Harvey off and away. The great sea closed over him, and he went quietly to sleep.

He was awoken by the sound of a dinner horn. It reminded him of the horn that would call him to supper at the summer school he had once attended in the Adirondacks. Slowly he remembered that he was Harvey Cheyne, drowned and dead in midocean, but he was too weak to fit things together. A new smell filled his nostrils; wet and clammy chills ran down his back, and he was helplessly full of salt water. When he opened his eyes, he saw that he was still on the top of the sea, for it was running around him in silver-colored hills. He was lying on a pile of half-dead fish, looking at a broad human back clothed in a blue jersey.

"It's no good," thought the boy. "I'm dead, sure enough, and this thing is in charge."

He groaned, and the figure turned its head,

showing a pair of little gold eyeglass rings half hidden in curly black hair.

"Aha! You feel some pretty well now?" it said. "Lie still so we float better."

With a swift jerk he steered the small boat head-on into the rough sea. The boat would rise up twenty full feet, only to slide back down again. But this mountain climbing did not interrupt blue jersey's talk. "Fine, good job, I say, that I catch you. Better good job, I say, your boat didn't catch me. How you come to fall out?"

"I was sick," said Harvey; "sick, and couldn't help it."

"Just in time I blow my horn to warn the ship, and your boat, she turned a little. Then I see you come down. I think you are cut into bits by the propellers, but you drift—drift to me and I fish you out. So you shall not die this time."

"Where am I?" said Harvey.

"You are with me in the dory—Manuel is my name, and I come from the fishing ship *We're Here* of Gloucester, Massachusetts. We get supper in a while."

Not content with blowing through a big conch shell, Manuel also felt the need to stand up in the "dory," which Harvey observed to be a small rowboat. Manuel swayed with the sway of the flat-bottomed dory, and sent a grinding, shuddering shriek through the fog. How long this entertainment lasted, Harvey could not remember, for he lay back terrified at the sight of the large waves. He thought he heard a gun and a horn and shouting. Something bigger than the dory, but just as noisy, loomed alongside. Several voices talked at once; he was dropped into a dark, heaving hole, where men dressed in waterproof oilskin coats gave him a hot drink and took off his clothes, and he fell asleep.

When he woke up, he listened for the breakfast bell on the passenger ship, wondering why his private room felt so small. Turning, he looked into a narrow, triangular cave, lit by a lamp. At the other end, behind an old wood-burning stove, sat a boy about his own age, with a flat red face and a pair of twinkling gray eyes. He was dressed in a blue jersey and high rubber boots.

Several pairs of the same sort of shoes, an old hat, and some worn-out wool socks lay on the floor, and black and yellow oilskins swayed to and fro beside the bunk beds. The place was filled with smells. The oilskins had a strangely thick scent of their own which made a sort of background to the smells of fried fish, burnt grease, paint, pepper, and stale tobacco; all mixed together by one encircling smell of salt water. Harvey saw with disgust that there were no sheets on his bed. He was lying on a piece of the lumpy cloth used to cover the smaller fishing dories. Then he noticed that the boat did not move like the passenger ship, which has a steam engine. She wasn't sliding or rolling, but rather, wriggling around. He could hear water noises, and the wood beams creaked around him. All these things made him grunt despairingly and think of his mother.

"Feelin' better?" said the boy, with a grin. "Hev some coffee?" He brought a full tin cup and sweetened it with molasses.

"Isn't there milk?" said Harvey, looking around the dark room as if he expected to find a cow there.

"Well, no," said the boy. "And there ain't likely to be till 'bout mid-September. It ain't bad coffee. I made it."

Harvey drank in silence, and the boy handed him a plate full of pieces of crisp fried pork, which he ate hungrily.

"I've dried your clothes. Guess they've shrunk some," said the boy. "They ain't our style much. Move 'round an' see if you're hurt anywhere."

Harvey stretched himself in every direction, but could not report any injuries.

"That's good," the boy said enthusiastically. "Get dressed an' go on deck. Dad wants to see you. I'm his son—Dan, they call me—and I'm the cook's helper an' everything else aboard that's too dirty for the men. There ain't no boy here 'cept me since Otto went overboard. How'd you come to fall off in a dead calm sea?"

"It wasn't calm," said Harvey, grumpily. "It was a storm, and I was seasick. Guess I must have rolled over the railing."

"There was a little bit o' waves yesterday an' last night," said the boy. "But if that's your idea of a storm . . ." He whistled. "You'll know better before you're through. Hurry! Dad's waitin'."

Like many other unfortunate young people, Harvey had never in all his life received a direct order—never, at least, without long, and sometimes tearful, explanations of why he should listen to his elders. Mrs. Cheyne lived in fear of breaking his spirit, which, perhaps, was the reason that she herself was always on the verge of breaking down. He could not see why he should be expected to hurry for anyone else, and said so. "Your dad can come down here if he's so anxious to talk to me. I want him to take me to New York right away. It'll pay him."

Dan opened his eyes as the size and beauty of this joke dawned on him. "Say, Dad!" he shouted to the upper deck, "He says you kin come down an' see him if you're that anxious. 'Hear, Dad?"

The answer came back in the deepest voice Harvey had ever heard from a human chest: "Quit foolin', Dan, and send him to me."

Dan snickered, and threw Harvey his warped bicycle shoes. There was something about the voice on deck that made Harvey hide his extreme rage. He consoled himself with the thought of gradually telling the story of his father's wealth on the voyage home. This rescue would certainly make him a hero among his friends. He hoisted himself on deck up a steep ladder, and stumbled forward over a variety of objects, to where a short, bulky, clean-shaven man with gray eyebrows sat on a step. The sea was calm again, and a dozen fishing ships floated on the horizon. Between them lay little black specks showing where the dories were out fishing. The schooner floated easily at anchor, and except for the man on the step, the boat was deserted.

"Mornin'—Good afternoon, I should say. You've nearly slept 'round the clock, young feller," was the greeting.

"Mornin'," said Harvey. He did not like being called "young feller," and, since he had been rescued from drowning, expected sympathy. His mother became hysterical if he even got his feet wet, but this man did not seem excited.

"Now let's hear all about it. It's quite lucky, for all concerned. What might be your name? Where from (we suspect it's Noo York), an' where to (we suspect it's Europe)?"

Harvey gave his name, the name of the steamer, and a short history of the accident. He then demanded to be taken to New York immediately, where his father would pay any amount anyone chose to name.

"Hmm," said the shaven man, quite unimpressed by the end of Harvey's speech. "I can't say we think special of any man, or boy even, that falls overboard from that kind o' ship in a flat, calm sea. Least of all when his excuse is that he's seasick."

"Excuse?!" cried Harvey. "D'you think I'd fall overboard into your dirty little boat for fun?"

"Not knowin' what your ideas of fun may be, I can't rightly say, young feller. But if I was you, I wouldn't call the boat that under God's good guidance, was the means of savin' your life, names. First, it's disrespectful to God. Second, it's annoying to my feelings—and I'm Disko Troop, captain o' the fishing vessel *We're Here* of Gloucester, Massachusetts, which you don't seem rightly to know."

"I don't know and I don't care," said Harvey. "I'm grateful enough for being saved

and all that, of course! But I want you to understand that the sooner you take me back to New
York, the better it'll pay you."

"Meanin'—how?" Troop raised one shaggy
eyebrow over a light blue eye.

"Dollars and cents," said Harvey, delighted
to think that he was making an impression.
"Cold dollars and cents." He shoved a hand into
a pocket, and pushed out his stomach a little,
which was his way of acting tough. "You've done
the best day's work you ever did in your life when
you pulled me out of the sea. I'm the only son
Harvey Cheyne has."

"He's been blessed," said Disko, rolling his
eyes.

"And if you don't know who Harvey Cheyne
is, you don't know much—that's all. Now turn
this boat around and let's hurry."

Harvey believed that most of America was
filled with people who knew his father, and were
jealous of his money.

"When do you suppose we shall get to New
York?"

"I don't sail through New York. We may see
Gloucester about September, an' your pa—I'm
real sorry I ain't never heard of him—may give
me ten dollars after all your talk. Then of course,
he may not."

"Ten dollars! Why, look here, I—" Harvey
dived into his pocket for the wad of bills. All he

brought up was a soggy packet of cigarettes.

"Not legal money, an' bad for the lungs. Toss 'em overboard, young feller, and try again."

"It's been stolen!" cried Harvey, angrily.

"You'll hev to wait till you see your pa to give me my reward, then?"

"A hundred and thirty-four dollars—all stolen," said Harvey, hunting wildly through his pockets. "Give them back."

Troop's hard face suddenly changed. "What might you be doin' at your age with one hundred an' thirty-four dollars, young feller?"

"It was part of my allowance—for a month." Harvey was sure this would impress Troop.

"Oh! One hundred and thirty-four dollars is only part of his allowance—for one month only! You don't remember hittin' your head when you fell over, do you? Old man Hasken"—Troop seemed to be talking to himself—"he tripped on his boat and hit his head hard. 'Bout three weeks afterwards, old man Hasken insisted that his fishing boat was a fightin' warship, an' so he declared war on Sable Island because it was British. They sewed him up in a bag, his head an' feet stickin' out, for the rest o' the trip, an' now he lives in a mental hospital playin' with little rag dolls."

Harvey choked with anger, but Troop went on consolingly: "We're sorry fer you. We're very sorry fer you—an' so young! We won't say no more about the money, I guess."

"'Course you won't. You stole it."

"Suit yourself. We stole it if it's any comfort to you. Now, about goin' back to New York. Allowin' we could do it, which we can't, you ain't in no good shape to go back to your home, and we've jest come to the Grand Banks, workin' fer our money. We don't see the half of a hundred dollars a month, let alone extra spending money. With good luck, we'll be ashore again somewhere around the first weeks o' September."

"But—but it's May now, and I can't stay here doin' nothing just because you want to fish. I can't, I tell you!"

"There's a heap 'o work to do since Otto went overboard. I think he lost his grip in a storm. Anyways, you've turned up, which is plain lucky for all of us. I suspect there's not much you can do, though. Ain't that so?"

"I can make it worthwhile for you and your crowd when we get ashore," said Harvey, with a fierce nod, murmuring vague threats about "thievery," at which Troop almost—not quite— smiled.

"Except talk. I'd forget that. Keep your eyes open, an' help Dan do as he's told. I'll give you— you ain't worth it, but I'll give—ten and a half dollars a month; say thirty-five at the end o' the trip. A little work will clear your head, and you kin tell us all about your dad an' your mom an' your money afterwards."

"She's on the steamer," said Harvey, his eyes filling with tears. "Take me to New York at once."

"Poor woman—poor woman! When she has you back she'll forget it all, though. There's eight of us on the *We're Here*, an' if we went back now—it's more'n a thousand miles—we'd lose a season's worth of pay. The men wouldn't allow it."

"But my father would make it all right."

"He'd try. I don't doubt he'd try," said Troop; "but a whole season's catch is eight men's pay, an' besides, you'll be stronger when you see him in the fall. Go help Dan. It's ten an' a half dollars a month, I said, an' o' course, you'll help with all the chores, same as the rest o' us."

"Do you mean I'm to clean pots and pans?" said Harvey.

"An' other things. You've no call to shout, young feller."

"I won't! My father will give you enough to buy this dirty little fishing boat ten times over"—Harvey stamped on the deck—"if you take me to New York safe. And—and—you owe me a hundred and thirty dollars anyhow."

"How do you figure that?" said Troop, his hard face darkening.

"How? You know how well enough! On top of all that, you want me to do maid's work till the fall. I tell you I will not! Understand?"

Troop looked up at the main mast of his ship

with deep interest for a while, as Harvey hollered fiercely all around him.

"Hush!" he said at last. "I'm figurin' out my responsibilities in my own mind. It's a matter o' judgment."

Dan sneaked up quietly and tugged at Harvey's elbow. "Careful what you say to my Dad," he pleaded. "You've called him a thief two or three times, an' he don't take that from any livin' being."

"I won't!" Harvey almost shrieked, ignoring the advice.

"Seems kind of unfriendly," Troop said at last, his eye traveling down to Harvey. "I— don't blame you fer being upset, not a bit, young feller, and you won't blame me when you're not so angry. Sure you understand what I say? Ten an' a half dollars for a second boy on the ship—and all chores—to teach you, and for the sake o' your health. Yes or no?"

"No!" said Harvey. "Take me back to New York or I'll—"

He did not exactly remember what followed. He was lying in the gutter of the ship, holding on to a bloody nose while Troop looked down on him calmly.

"Dan," he said to his son, "I was set against this young feller when I first saw him on account o' my hasty judgment. Don't you ever be led astray by hasty judgments, Dan. Now I'm sorry for him, because he's confused in the head. He ain't responsible for the names he called me, nor for the other things he said, nor for jumpin' overboard, which I'm about half convinced he did. You be gentle with him, Dan, or I'll give you twice what I give him. Bleeding clears the head. Let him clean it out!"

Troop went down into the cabin, leaving Dan to comfort the unlucky heir to thirty million.

CHAPTER 2

"**I** warned ye," said Dan, as the drops of blood fell thick and fast on the dark, oiled deck of the ship. "There's no sense talkin' on so." Harvey's shoulders were rising and falling in spasms of dry sobbing. "I know the feelin'. First time Dad knocked me out was the last—and that was my first trip. Makes ye feel sick and lonesome. I know."

"It does," moaned Harvey. "That man's either crazy or drunk, and—and I can't do anything."

"Don't say that to Dad," whispered Dan. "He's set against all liquor, and—well, he told me you was the madman. What made you call him a thief? He's my dad."

Harvey sat up, mopped his nose, and told the story of the missing wad of bills. "I'm not crazy," he said. "Only—your father has never seen more than a five-dollar bill at a time, and my father could buy up this boat once a week and never miss it."

"You don't know what the *We're Here*'s worth. Your dad must have a pile o' money. How did he git it?"

"He has gold mines and things, out West."

"I've read about that kind o' business. Out West, too? Does he go around with a pistol on a pony and do tricks, same as the circus? They call that the Wild West."

"You are a chump!" said Harvey, amused in spite of himself. "My father hasn't any use for ponies. When he wants to ride, he takes his private train car."

"What train car?"

"His own private train car, of course. You've seen a private car some time in your life?"

"Slatin Beeman has one," said Dan, cautiously. "I saw it in Boston once. But Slatin Beeman, they say he owns 'bout every railroad on Long Island. They say he's bought 'bout half of Noo Hampshire. Slatin Beeman, he's a millionaire. I've seen his car. Yes?"

"Well, my father's what they call a multi-millionaire, and he has two private cars. One's named for me, the *Harvey*, and one for my mother, the *Constance*."

"Hold on," said Dan. "Dad don't ever let me swear, but I guess you can. Before we go ahead, I want you to say that you hope you will die if you're lyin'."

"Of course," said Harvey.

"That ain't enough. Say, 'Hope I will die if I ain't speakin' truth."

"Hope I will die right here," said Harvey, "if every word I've spoken isn't the cold truth."

"Even the hundred an' thirty-four dollars?" said Dan. "I heard you talkin' to Dad, an' I half expected you'd be swallowed up by a whale fer lyin', same as Jonah in the Bible."

Harvey protested until he was red in the face. Dan was a smart young person, and ten minutes of questioning convinced him that Harvey was not lying—much. Besides, he had bound himself by the most terrible oath known to boyhood, and yet he sat, alive, with a bloody nose, recounting marvels upon marvels.

"Gosh!" said Dan at last from the very bottom of his soul when Harvey had described the train car named in his honor. Then a grin of mischievous delight spread across his broad face. "I believe you, Harvey. Dad's made a mistake fer once in his life."

"He has," said Harvey, who was plotting an early revenge.

"He'll sure be mad. Dad just hates to be mistook in his judgments." Dan lay back and slapped his thigh. "Oh, Harvey, don't you spoil it by lettin' on."

"I don't want to be knocked down again. I'll get even with him, though."

"Never heard of any man who got even with Dad. But he'd knock ye down again for sure. The more he was mistaken, the more he'd do it. But gold mines and pistols—"

"I never said a word about pistols," Harvey cut in.

"That's true. Two private train cars, then, one named for you an' one for her; an' two hundred a month pocket money, all knocked into the gutter for not workin' for ten an' a half dollars a month!" He exploded with noiseless chuckles.

"Then I was right to get mad?" said Harvey, who thought he had found someone who agreed with him.

"You was wrong! The wrongest kind of wrong! You better pitch in alongside of me, or you'll get it from Dad, an' I'll get it for backin' you up. Dad always gives me double punishment 'cause I'm his son, and he hates favorin' folk. 'Guess you're kinda mad at dad. I've been that way time an' again. But Dad's a mighty fair man. All the men say so."

"Does this look fair to you?" Harvey pointed to his outraged nose.

"That's nothin'. Dad did it for your health. Say, though, I can't work with a man that thinks me or Dad or anyone on the *We're Here* is a thief. We ain't just any common crowd. We're fishermen, an' we've shipped together for six years an' more. Don't you make any mistake about that! I told you Dad don't let me swear. But if I could, I'd swear that no one took your money. I dunno what was in your pockets when I dried your

clothes since I didn't look to see. But I'd swear
—using the very same words you used about
your pa—that neither me nor Dad knows anythin' 'bout the money. And we was the only two
that touched you after you was brought aboard.
That's my say."

The bleeding had certainly cleared Harvey's
brain, and maybe the loneliness of the sea had
something to do with it. "That's all right," he
said. Then he looked down confusedly. "Seems
to me that for a fellow just saved from drowning,
I haven't been very grateful, Dan."

"Well, you was shook up and confused," said
Dan. "Anyway, there was only Dad an' me
aboard to see it."

"I might have thought about losing the
money when I went overboard," Harvey said,
half to himself, "instead of calling everybody a
thief. Where's your father?"

"In the cabin. What do you want with him
again?"

"You'll see," said Harvey, and he stepped,
rather slowly, for his head was still spinning, to
the cabin steps. Troop, in the chocolate-and-yel-
low painted cabin, was busy with a notebook and
an enormous black pencil, which he would suck
on loudly from time to time.

"I haven't acted quite right," said Harvey,
surprised at his own humility.

"What's wrong now?" asked Troop.

"Well, I—I'm here to take things back," said Harvey very quickly. "When a man's saved from drowning—" he gulped.

"Well! You might still become a man if you go on this way."

"He shouldn't begin by calling people names."

"That's right," said Troop, with a dry smile.

"So I'm here to say I'm sorry." Another big gulp.

Troop heaved himself slowly off the locker he was sitting on and held out an eleven inch hand. "I thought you'd come around, an' this shows I wasn't mistook in my judgments." A smothered chuckle on deck caught his ear. "I am very seldom wrong in my judgments." The eleven inch hand closed on Harvey's wrist, numbing it to the elbow. "We'll put a little more meat on that before we're done with you, young feller. An' I don't think any worse of you for anythin' that's been said. You wasn't responsible. Just go about your business an' you won't get hurt anymore."

Harvey returned to the deck, flushed to the tips of his ears.

"I heard what Dad said," said Dan. "He hates to be wrong in his judgments. Once Dad makes a judgment, he'd rather turn British than change it. Dad's right when he says he can't take you back to New York. Fishin's all the money we make. The men'll be back in half an hour—like sharks after a dead whale."

"What for?" said Harvey.

"Supper, o' course. Don't your stomach tell you? You've got a lot to learn."

"Guess I have," said Harvey, miserably, looking up at the tangle of ropes and sails overhead.

"She's a beauty," said Dan enthusiastically, misunderstanding the look. "Wait till our main sail is up, an' she glides home to Gloucester with her belly full. There's some work to do first, though." He pointed down into the darkness of the open main hatch, a huge storage compartment between the two large masts that supported the sails.

"What's that for? It's all empty," said Harvey.

"You and me and the other men hev to fill it," said Dan. "That's where the fish go."

"Alive?" said Harvey.

"Well, no. They're supposed to be rather

dead—an' flat—an' packed in salt. There's a hundred barrels o' salt down there."

"Where are the fish, though?"

"'In the sea they say, in the boats we pray,'" said Dan, quoting a fisherman's saying. "You came in last night with about forty of 'em."

He pointed to a sort of wooden pen that sat just in front of the storage hold.

"You an' me will wash that out when they're through. I've seen those pens filled up to half a foot with fish waitin' to be cut open and cleaned. We stood at the tables till we was cuttin' ourselves instead o' the fish, we was so sleepy. Yes, they're coming in now." Dan looked over the side of the ship at half a dozen dories rowing towards them over the shining, silky sea.

"I've never seen the sea from so low down," said Harvey. "It's beautiful."

The low sun made the water all purple and pinkish, with golden lights on the tops of the long waves. Each schooner in sight seemed to be pulling her dories towards her by invisible strings, and the little black figures in the tiny boats pulled like little toys.

"Looks like a good catch," said Dan, between his half-shut eyes. "Manuel ain't got room for another fish."

"Which is Manuel? I don't see how you can tell 'em apart from so far way."

"Last boat to the south. He found you last

night," said Dan, pointing. "Manuel's from Portugal. He rows different than the others; ye can't mistake him. East o' him is the man we call Pennsylvania. East o' him, with the humpy shoulders, is Long Jack. He's from Galway, Ireland, but now he lives in South Boston, where they all live mostly. North, away in the distance, is Tom Platt. You'll hear him git to singin' in a minute. He was on the *Ohio,* first ship of our navy, he says, to go 'round Cape Horn at the tip of South America. He never talks about much else, 'cept when he sings, but he has good fishin' luck. There! What did I tell you?"

Harvey could hear a pleasant voice singing across the water from the northern dory:

And now to thee, O Captain,
Most earnestly I pray,
That they shall never bury me
In church or graveyard gray.

"Tom will tell you all about the old *Ohio* tomorrow. See that blue dory behind him? He's my uncle, Dad's own brother, an' if there's any bad luck loose on the Grand Banks it'll find Uncle Salters, for sure. Look how carefully he's rowin'. I bet he's the only man who got stung today, and he's stung up good."

"What'll sting him?" asked Harvey, getting interested.

"Jellyfish, mostly. Strawberry-bottoms and such. Yep, he's stung up from his elbows down.

That man's luck is perfectly terrible. Now we'll take a-hold of the tackles an' hoist in the dories. Is it true what you told me just now, that you never done a day of work in all your born life? Must feel kinda awful, don't it?"

"I'm going to try to work, anyway," Harvey replied in a determined voice. "Only it's all new to me."

"Get a-hold of that tackle, then. Behind you!"

Harvey grabbed the "tackle"—a series of ropes and long iron hooks dangling from the main mast—while Dan pulled down another that ran from something he called a "topping lift." Manuel rowed alongside in his loaded dory and smiled a brilliant smile at Harvey. Then, with a short-handled fork, he began to throw fish into the pen on deck. "Two hundred and thirty-one," he shouted.

"Give him the hook," said Dan, and Harvey ran it into Manuel's hands. He slipped it through a loop of rope at the front of the dory, caught Dan's tackle, hooked it to the back of the boat, and climbed into the schooner.

"Pull!" shouted Dan, and Harvey pulled, astonished to find how easily the dory rose.

"Hold on!" Dan laughed, and Harvey held on, for the boat swung in the air above his head.

"Lower away," Dan shouted, and as Harvey lowered, Dan swayed the light boat with one hand till it landed softly just behind the main mast. "They don't weigh nuthin' empty."

"Ah ha!" said Manuel, holding out a brown hand. "You feel pretty well now? This time last night, the fish was fishing for you. Now you fish for fish."

"I'm—I'm ever so grateful," Harvey stammered, and his hand slipped to his pocket once more, but he remembered that he had no money to offer. When he knew Manuel better, the mere thought of the mistake he almost made would make him flush with embarrassment.

"There is nothin' to thank me for!" said Manuel. "How can I let you drift, drift all around the Banks? Now you are a fisherman!? Oh! Ouch!" He bent backward and forward stiffly to get the kinks out of his body.

"I have not cleaned boat today. Too busy. The fish, they came on quick. Danny, my son, clean for me."

Harvey moved forward at once. Here was something he could do for the man who had saved his life.

Dan threw him a mop, and he leaned over the dory, mopping up the slime clumsily. "Pull out the footboards," said Dan. He pointed to the boards of wood that lined the bottom of the boat. "Swab 'em an' lay 'em down on deck. Never let a footboard get stuck. You may need her bad some day. Here's Long Jack."

A stream of glittering fish flew into the pen from a dory alongside.

"Manuel, you take the tackle. I'll fix the tables. Harvey, clear Manuel's boat. We'll put Long Jack's dory on top o' her."

Harvey looked up from his mopping, or "swabbing" as Dan called it. He saw the bottom of another dory just above his head.

"Jus' like a puzzle, ain't it?" said Dan, as one boat dropped into the other.

"Boy takes to it like a duck to water," said Long Jack, an Irishman with a messy gray beard, bending to and fro exactly as Manuel had done to stretch out his body. Disko, who was still sitting in the cabin, growled up the stairs to the men. They could hear him suck his pencil.

"One hundred an' forty-nine, Disko!" said Long Jack. "I'm murderin' meself to fill your pockets."

Another dory came alongside, and more fish shot into the pen.

"Two hundred and three. Let's look at the passenger!" The speaker was even larger than the Irishman. A purple scar ran across his face, from his left eye to the right corner of his mouth.

Not knowing what else to do, Harvey swabbed each dory as it came down, pulled out the footboards, and laid them on deck.

"He's caught on good," said the scarred man, who was Tom Platt. He watched Harvey carefully. "There are two ways of doin' everything. One's the fisherman way, and the other's . . ."

"What we did on the old *Ohio!*" Dan interrupted, barging into the crowd of men. He carried a long wooden board with legs. "Get out o' here, Tom Platt, an' let me fix the tables."

He jammed one end of the board into two slots in the side of the boat, kicked out the leg, and ducked just in time to avoid a punch from Tom, the navy man.

"They did that on the *Ohio,* too, Danny. See?" said Tom Platt, laughing.

"Well, I know who'll find his boots hangin' from the mast if he don't leave us alone. Out of my way! I'm busy, can't ye see?"

"Danny, ye lie around an' sleep all day," said Long Jack. "I'm sure ye'll corrupt our new passenger in a week."

"His name's Harvey," said Dan, waving two strangely shaped knives, "an' he'll be better than five of ye South Boston clam diggers 'fore long." He laid the knives carefully on the table.

"I think it's forty-two," said a small voice from the water, and there was a roar of laughter as another voice answered, "Then my luck's turned good for once, 'cuz I'm at forty-five. I'm stung all over though."

"Forty-two or forty-five. I've lost count," the voice said timidly.

"It's Pennsylvania an' Uncle Salters countin' their catch. This beats the circus any day," said Dan. "Just look at 'em!"

"Forty-two, ye said." This was Uncle Salters.

"I'll count again, then," the voice replied weakly. The two dories swung together and smacked into the schooner's side.

"Careful!" snapped Uncle Salters. "What possessed a farmer like you to set foot in a boat beats me. Ye nearly smashed my boat to bits."

"I am sorry, Mr. Salters. I came to sea on account of my nervous stomach condition. You advised me, I think."

"You an' your nervis stomach be drowned," roared Uncle Salters, a fat and tubby little man. "Ye gonna hit me boat again. Did ye say forty-two or forty-five?"

"I've forgotten, Mr. Salters. Let's count."

"Don't see how it could be forty-five. I'm forty-five," said Uncle Salters. "Count carefully, Penn."

Disko Troop came out of the cabin. "Salters, you throw your fish up here right now," he said in the tone of authority.

"Don't spoil it, Dad," Dan murmured. "Them two are only just beginnin'."

"My God! He's throwin' them fish one by one," howled Long Jack, as Uncle Salters got to work. The little man in the other dory counted a line of notches on the side of his boat.

"That was last week's catch," he said, looking up with a confused expression. He kept his finger on the notch where he had finished counting.

Manuel nudged Dan, who darted to the tackle, and, leaning far over the side of the ship, slipped the hooks into the dory's ropes. The others pulled strongly and swung the boat on deck —man, fish, and all.

"One, two, four-nine," said Tom Platt as he quickly counted the fish. "Forty-seven. Penn, you're it!" Dan let the ropes loosen and slid Pennsylvania out of the boat, onto the deck, along with a pile of his own fish.

"Hold on!" roared Uncle Salters, who was now hanging onto his boat. "Hold on, I'm a bit mixed up in my count."

He had no time to protest, but was hoisted onboard like Penn.

"Forty-one," said Tom Platt. "Beat by a farmer, Salters. An' you such a sailor, too!"

"It wasn't a fair count," said he, stumbling to his feet; "an' I'm stung up all to pieces."

His thick hands were puffy and purple-white.

"Some folks will find jellyfish," said Dan, addressing the newly risen moon, "if they hev to dive for 'em."

"An' others," said Uncle Salters, "lay 'round like lazy do-nuthin's, an' make fun o' their own family."

"Supper! Supper!" a voice called from the lower deck at the front of the ship. Harvey had not heard the voice before. Disko Troop, Tom Platt, Long Jack and Salters went forward at once. Little

Penn bent over his tangled fishing lines; Manuel lay down full length on the deck, and Dan dropped into the storage hold, where Harvey heard him banging barrels with a hammer.

"Salt," he said, returning. "Soon as supper's done, we git to dressin' down the fish. That means cut 'em, clean 'em, and stow 'em in salt. You'll throw the fish to Dad. Tom Platt an' Dad, they pack the fish together down below, an' you'll hear 'em arguin'. We're what you call the 'second half'. We eat supper second, you an' me an' Manuel an' Penn—the youth an' beauty of the boat."

"What's the good of that?" said Harvey. "I'm hungry."

"They'll be through in a minute. Mmm! Smells good tonight. It's a full catch today, ain't it?" He pointed at the wooden pens piled high with codfish. "How deep did ye fish, Manuel?"

"Twenty-five fathom," said the Portuguese, sleepily. Harvey learned later that a "fathom" equaled six feet. "The fish, they came on good an' quick. Some day I show you, Harvey."

The moon was beginning to walk on the still sea before the older men came back from dinner. The cook had no need to yell "second half." Dan and Manuel were down the hatch and at the table before Tom Platt, last and slowest of the elders, had finished wiping his mouth with the back of his hand. Harvey followed Penn, and sat down before a tin pan of cod tongues mixed with scraps of pork and fried potato, a loaf of hot bread, and some black and powerful coffee. Hungry as they were, they waited while Pennsylvania said a blessing. Then they ate in silence till Dan took a breath over his tin cup and asked Harvey how he felt.

"'Almost full, but there's just room for another piece."

The cook was a huge and quiet black man that the men had nicknamed "doctor," since he fed them and therefore, made them feel much better at the end of a long day. He didn't speak much and seemed content to simply smile and gesture for the men to eat more.

"See, Harvey," said Dan, tapping with his fork on the table, "it's just as I said. The young an' handsome men—like me an' Penn an' you an' Manuel—we're second half, an' we eat when the first half are through. They're the old fish; an' they're mean an' grumpy, an' their stummicks have to be happy; so they come first, which they don't deserve. Ain't that so, doctor?"

The cook nodded.

"Can't he talk?" said Harvey in a whisper.

"Enough to get along. Not much o' anything we understand. His way o' speakin' is strange. Comes from Cape Breton, Canada, he does, where the farmers speak their own kind 'o Scottish. Cape Breton's full o' blacks who escaped there durin' our war."

"That is not Scottish," said Penn. "That is Gaelic. So I read in a book."

"Penn reads a heap. Most of what he says is right—'cept when it comes to a count o' fish."

"Does your father just let them say how many they've caught without checking them?" said Harvey.

"Why, yes. What's the sense of a man lyin' fer a few old cod?"

"Once knew a man who lied for his catch," Manuel said. "Lied every day. Five, ten, twenty-five more fish than there was."

"Where was that?" said Dan. "None of our folk."

"Frenchman."

"Ah! Them Frenchmen can't count anyway," said Dan, with an awful contempt.

Long Jack hollered down the hatch, and the "second half" scrambled up at once.

In the moonlight, the shadows of the huge masts rolled back and forth on the heaving deck. The pile of fish sparkled like liquid silver. In the storage hold there were grunts and rumblings where Disko Troop and Tom Platt moved among the salt barrels. Dan passed Harvey a pitchfork, and led him to the end of the rough table, where Uncle Salters was drumming a knife impatiently. A tub of salt water lay at his feet.

"You pitch to Dad an' Tom Platt down the hatch, an' careful Uncle Salters don't cut yer eye out," said Dan, swinging himself down into the storage hold. "I'll pass salt below."

Penn and Manuel stood knee-deep among cod in the pen, with drawn knives. Long Jack, a basket at his feet and mittens on his hands, faced Uncle Salters at the table, and Harvey stared at the pitchfork and the tub.

"Eye!" shouted Manuel, crouching among the fish, and bringing one up with a finger under its gill and a finger in its eyes. He laid it on the edge of the pen and the knife blade made a ripping sound. Then the fish, split from end to end, with a cut on either side of the neck, dropped at Long Jack's feet.

"Eye!" said Long Jack, with a scoop of his hand. The cod's liver dropped in the basket. Another scoop sent the head flying, and the empty fish slid across to Uncle Salters, who snorted fiercely. There was another sound of tearing. The backbone flew over the side of the ship, and the fish, headless, gutted, and open, splashed in the tub, sending the salt water into Harvey's astonished mouth. After the first yell, the men were silent. The cod moved along as though they were alive, and before Harvey knew it, his tub was full. He was amazed at the skill and speed of the fisherman.

"Pitch!" grunted Uncle Salters, without turning his head, and Harvey tossed the fish by twos and threes down the hatch.

"Pitch 'em all together," shouted Dan. "Don't scatter 'em! Uncle Salters is the best splitter in the fleet. Watch him!"

Indeed, the fat uncle cut open the fish with astounding speed and skill. Manuel's body, bent over from the hips, stayed completely still. But his long arms grabbed the fish without stopping. Little Penn tried his best, but it was easy to see he was weak. Once or twice Manuel found time to help him without slowing down the other men.

At the end of an hour Harvey would have given the world to rest. Fresh, wet cod weigh more than you would think, and his back ached with the steady pitching. But he felt for the first time in his life that he was one of the working gang of men, took pride in the thought, and held on.

"Knife oh!" shouted Uncle Salters at last. Penn stood up slowly, gasping among the fish, Manuel bowed back and forth to stretch himself, and Long Jack leaned over the side of the boat. The cook appeared, quiet as a shadow, collected a mass of backbones and heads, and retreated.

"Fish head chowder for breakfast," said Long Jack, smacking his lips.

"Knife oh!" repeated Uncle Salters, waving the flat, curved splitter's weapon.

"Look by your foot, Harve," cried Dan below.

Harvey saw half a dozen knives stuck in the

wood by the hatch. He gave these to the men, taking their dulled knives in return.

"Water!" said Disko Troop.

"Drinkin' water's at the front of the boat. Hurry, Harve," said Dan.

He was back in a minute with a big cup of stale brown water which tasted like honey. He gave this to Disko and Tom Platt.

"Eye!" With a yell from Manuel the work began again, and never stopped till the pen was empty. The instant the last fish was down, Disko Troop retreated to the cabin with his brother; Manuel and Long Jack walked forward to their bunks; Tom Platt only waited long enough to secure the hatch before he, too, disappeared. In half a minute Harvey heard deep snores in the cabin, and he was staring blankly at Dan and Penn.

"I did a little better that time, Danny," said Penn, whose eyelids were heavy with sleep. "But I think it is my duty to help clean."

"Go to bed, Penn," said Dan. "You've no reason to do boy's work. Bring me a bucket of water, Harvey. Oh, Penn, take care o' these before you sleep. Kin you keep awake that long?"

Penn picked up the heavy basket of fish livers and emptied them into a barrel; then he too dropped out of sight in the cabin.

"Boys clean up after the dressin' down o' the fish. And in calm weather, we take first watch."

Dan rinsed the pen energetically, dismantled the table and set it up to dry in the moonlight. He then wiped the red knife blades through a wad of old rope strings and began to sharpen them on a tiny grindstone. Harvey threw backbones overboard under Dan's direction.

At the first splash, a silvery-white ghost bolted upright from the oily water and sighed a weird whistling sigh. Harvey jumped back with a shout, but Dan only laughed.

"Orca whale," he said. "Beggin' for fish heads. They jump up that way when they're hungry. Terrible breath on him, ain't it?" A horrible stench of decayed fish filled the air as the pillar of white sank and the water bubbled. "Ain't ye never seen a whale jump up before? You'll see hundreds of 'em before you're through. Say, it's good to hev a boy aboard again. Otto was too old. Him and me, we fought a lot. You sleepy?"

"Dead sleepy," said Harvey, nodding forward.

"Mustn't sleep on watch. Wake up an' see if our anchor light's bright an' shining so the other ships can see us. You're on watch now, Harve." Dan pointed to the white light that shone brightly on the masthead.

"Oh, what's to hurt us? It's bright as day. Snooore!"

"That's just when bad things happen, Dad says. Fine weather makes for good sleepin', an' before you know it, maybe you're cut in two by a passin' ship. Harve, I kinda like you, but if you nod off one more time, I'll whup you with the end of a rope."

The moon, who sees many strange things on the Grand Banks, looked down on a slim youth in short pants and a red shirt, staggering around the cluttered decks of a seventy-ton schooner. Behind him, waving a knotted rope like an executioner, walked a boy who yawned and nodded between the blows he dealt.

The steering wheel of the ship was tied in place and groaned softly. A small sail fluttered in the light wind. Harvey cursed, threatened, whimpered, and at last wept. Meanwhile, Dan spoke of the importance of staying alert and slashed away with the rope's end, punishing the dories as often as he hit Harvey. At last the clock in the cabin struck ten, and little Penn crept on deck. He found the two boys in two heaps, side by side on the deck, so deeply asleep that he actually rolled them to their bunks.

CHAPTER 3

After a deep sleep, the boys woke up starving. They emptied a big tin dish of juicy fish fragments that the cook had collected overnight. They cleaned up the plates and pans from the older men's breakfast, who were already out fishing. Then they sliced pork for the midday meal, swabbed down the deck, filled the lamps with oil, and drew coal and water for the cook. It was another perfect day, soft, mild, and clear, and Harvey breathed to the very bottom of his lungs.

More schooners had crept up in the night, and the long blue seas were full of sails and dories. Far away on the horizon, the smoke of a steam ship smudged the blue. Disko Troop was smoking a pipe by the roof of the cabin. He kept one eye on the ships around him. The other he kept on a "fly"—a small device that measures wind direction.

"Dad's doin' some first-rate thinkin'," said Dan in a whisper. "I bet we set sail soon. Dad knows the cod, an' the other boats know that Dad knows. See 'em coming up one by one, lookin' fer nothin' in particular, o' course, but gatherin' around us all the time? There's the ship called the *Prince Leboo*. She's from Chatham, Massachusetts. She crept up on us last night. An' see that big one with a patch in her sail? She's the *Carrie Pitman* from West Chatham. Her sails won't last long, unless her luck changed since last season. She don't do much except drift. When the smoke puffs up in little rings like that, Dad's studyin' the fish. If we speak to him now, he'll git mad. Las' time I did, he threw a boot at me."

Disko Troop stared at the sea, the pipe between his teeth. As his son said, he was studying the fish—using his knowledge and experience on the Banks to locate the wandering cod. He accepted the presence of the curious schooners on the horizon as a compliment to his powers. But now he wished to make his way alone. So Disko Troop thought of the recent weather and storms, and which way the currents flowed in the ocean, all from the point of view of a twenty-pound cod. Then he removed the pipe from his teeth. "Dad," said Dan, "we've done our chores. Can't we go out in a dory for a while? It's good catchin' weather."

"Not in that cherry-colored outfit, or in them half-baked brown shoes. Give him sumthin' fit to wear."

"Dad's pleased—that settles it," said Dan, delightedly, dragging Harvey into the cabin, while Troop threw a key down the steps. "Dad keeps my spare clothes locked up, 'cause Ma sez I'm careless." He rummaged through a locker, and in less than three minutes Harvey was adorned with fisherman's rubber boots that came halfway up his thigh, a heavy blue shirt well worn at the elbows, a pair of thick gloves, and an oil-skin coat.

"Now ye look like somethin'," said Dan. "Hurry!"

"Don't go visitin' with the other ships," said Troop. "If anyone asks ye what I'm plannin' to do, speak the truth— ye don't know."

A little red dory, labeled "Hattie S." floated alongside the schooner. Dan hauled in the rope that tied the little boat to the schooner, and lightly dropped into the bottom. Harvey tumbled clumsily after him.

"That's no way o' gettin' into a boat," said Dan. "If the sea was makin' waves at all, you'd go to the bottom, for sure."

Dan slid the oars into their grooves on the side of the dory, and sat back to watch Harvey work. The boy had rowed on the small Adirondack ponds where he would vacation in the summer. But there's a difference between the light oars of a row boat, and the eight-foot sea oars he now tried to manage. They stuck in the water, and Harvey grunted.

"Short! Row short! Make short strokes!" said

Dan. "If your oar gets stuck in any kind o' bad weather, you're likely to flip her over. Ain't she a beauty? She's mine, too."

The little dory was spotlessly clean. At the bottom lay a tiny anchor and two jugs of water. A tin dinner horn rested just under Harvey's right hand, beside an ugly-looking hammer, a short iron hook, and a shorter wooden stick. There were also a couple of fishing lines and double cod hooks, all neatly coiled on square reels.

"Where's the sail and mast?" asked Harvey, whose hands were beginning to blister.

Dan chuckled. "You don't sail fishin' dories much. You pull 'em; but you don't need to pull so hard on them oars. Don't you wish you owned her?"

"Well, I guess my father might give me one or two if I asked him," Harvey replied. He had been too busy to think of his family much until then.

"That's so. I forgot your dad's a millionaire. You don't act very millionary now. But a dory and fishin' gear costs a heap." Dan spoke as though she were a whaleboat. "Think your dad 'u'd give you one for—for like a pet?"

"Shouldn't wonder. It'd be the only thing I haven't asked him for yet."

"Must be an expensive kind o' kid. Don't slither 'round that way, Harve. Short strokes is the trick, because no sea's ever dead still, an' the waves'll—"

Crack! The oar kicked Harvey under the chin and knocked him backwards.

"That was what I was goin' to say. I had to learn too, but I wasn't more than eight years old when I got my schoolin'."

Harvey regained his seat with aching jaws and a frown.

"No good gettin' mad at things, Dad says. It's our own fault if we can't handle 'em, he says. Let's try here. Manuel 'll give us the water."

Manuel was floating a full mile away, but when Dan held up an oar he waved his left arm three times.

"Thirty fathom," said Dan, stringing a salt clam on to the hook. "Bait the same way I do, Harvey, an' don't tangle your reel."

Dan's fishing line was out long before Harvey had mastered the mystery of baiting. The dory drifted along easily. It was not worthwhile to anchor until they were sure of good fishing water.

"Here we come!" Dan shouted, and a shower of spray rattled on Harvey's shoulders as a big cod flapped and kicked alongside.

"Muckle, Harvey, muckle! Under your hand! Quick!"

Harvey guessed that "muckle" could not be the dinner horn, so he passed over the hammer, and Dan scientifically stunned the fish before he pulled it onboard. He wrenched out the hook with the short wooden stick he called a "gob stick." Then Harvey felt a tug, and pulled up excitedly.

"Why, these are jellyfish!" he shouted. "Look!"

The hook had stuck among a bunch of "strawberry-bottom" jellyfish, red on one side and white on the other. They looked exactly like the fruit, except that there were no leaves, and the stem was all slimy.

"Don't touch 'em. Scrape 'em off. Don't—"

The warning came too late. Harvey had picked them from the hook, and was admiring them.

"Ouch!" he cried, for his fingers throbbed like he had grabbed a handful of thorns.

"Now ye know what a strawberry-bottom is. Nothin' 'cept fish should be touched with the naked fingers, Dad says. Scrape 'em off and bait up, Harve. Lookin' won't help any. It's all in the pay."

Harvey smiled at the thought of his ten and a half dollars a month, and wondered what his mother would say if she could see him hanging over the edge of a fishing dory in mid-ocean. She would worry herself sick whenever he went out on the lake where they used to vacation. Harvey remembered clearly that he used to laugh at her anxieties. Suddenly the fishing line zipped through his hand, stinging even through the heavy gloves that were supposed to protect it.

"He's a big one. Give him room accordin' to his strength," cried Dan. "I'll help ye."

"No, you won't," Harvey snapped, as he hung on to the line. "It's my first fish. I—is it a whale?"

"Halibut, maybe." Dan peered down into the water and held the big "muckle," ready to strike. Something white and oval flickered and fluttered in the water. "I'll bet he's over a hundred pounds. Sure you want to land him alone?"

Harvey's knuckles were raw and bleeding where they had banged against the boat. His face was purple-blue from excitement and strain. He dripped with sweat, and was half-blinded from staring at the sunlit water where his fishing line jerked and darted. The boys were tired long before the halibut, who took charge of them and the dory for the next twenty minutes. But the big flat fish was hauled in at last.

"Beginner's luck," said Dan, wiping his forehead. "He's a full hundred pounds."

Harvey looked at the huge gray creature with tremendous pride. He had seen halibut many times on shore, lined up on marble slabs, waiting to be bought. But it had never occurred to him to ask how they came inland. Now he knew, and every inch of his body ached with fatigue.

"If Dad was here," said Dan, "he'd read the signs. The fish are smaller an' smaller, an' you've probably caught the biggest halibut we'll find this trip. Yesterday's catch—did ye notice it?—was all big fish an' no halibut. Dad, he'd read them signs right off. Dad says everythin' on the Banks is signs, an' can be read wrong or right. Dad's deeper'n a whale."

Even as he spoke, someone fired a pistol on the *We're Here*.

"What did I say? That's the call for the whole crowd. Dad's onto somethin', or he'd never call the dories back this time o' day. Reel in your line, Harve, an' we'll head back."

They were almost to the schooner when the sounds of hollering a half mile off led them to Penn, who was careening around in a circle. The little man tried to row with enormous energy, but his dory would only swing around again and catch on her rope.

"We'll hev to help him," said Dan.

"What's the matter?" said Harvey. This was a new world, where he could not lay down the law to his elders, but had to ask questions humbly. And the sea was horribly big and indifferent.

"Anchor's stuck. Penn's always losing his anchor. Lost two this trip already. Dad says the next one he loses, he'll give him the kelleg. That'd break Penn's heart."

"What's a 'kelleg'?" said Harvey, who had a vague idea it might be some kind of marine torture.

"A big stone instead of an anchor. You can spot a kelleg in a dory from far off, and all the fishermen know what it means. They'd tease him somethin' awful. Penn couldn't stand that, he's so sensitive. Hello, Penn! Stuck again?"

"It doesn't move," said the little man, panting. "It doesn't move at all, and I tried everything."

Dan bent low over the front of Penn's dory to hide a smile, pulled once or twice on the rope, and the anchor appeared at once.

"Start rowin', Penn," he said laughing, "or she'll git stuck again."

They left him looking at the little anchor with big, pathetic blue eyes, and thanking them repeatedly.

"Oh, say, while I think of it, Harve," said Dan when they were far enough away that Penn couldn't hear them. "Penn ain't quite all there. He ain't dangerous or nuthin', but his mind gives out. Understand?"

"Is that right, or is it one of your father's judgments?" Harvey asked as he returned to his oars. He felt that he was learning how to handle them more easily.

"Dad ain't wrong this time. Penn's a loony, sure enough. No, he ain't that exactly, so much as a harmless idiot (you're rowin' good, Harve). I'm tellin' ye 'cause it's only right you know. He was a preacher once—with the Moravian Christians. Jacob Boiler wuz his name, Dad told me, an' he lived with his wife an' four children somewheres in Pennsylvania. Well, Penn took his family along to a Moravian meeting an' they stayed over just one night in Johnstown. You've heard talk o' Johnstown?"

Harvey thought for a moment. "Yes, I have. But I don't know why."

"Well, on that one single night, Johnstown was wiped out. The dam broke an' flooded the town, an' the houses began to float an' bumped into each other an' sunk. I've seen the pictures, an' they're dreadful. Penn saw his family drowned all in a heap before he even knew what was happenin'. His mind gave out from then on. He knew somethin' had happened up in Johnstown, but for the poor life of him he couldn't remember what. He just wandered around smilin' an' wonderin'. He didn't know who he was or what he had been. Then he run into Uncle Salters, who was visitin' Allegheny City. Half my mother's family lives scattered inside o' Pennsylvania, an' Uncle Salters visits around winter time. Uncle Salters, he sort of adopted Penn, knowin' what his trouble wuz; an' he brought him home, an' gave him work on his farm."

"Why, I heard him calling Penn a farmer last night when their boats bumped. Is your Uncle Salters a farmer?"

"Farmer?!" shouted Dan. "You bet he's a farmer. Best there is. He and Penn, they ran the farm together. Uncle Salters sold it this spring to a man from Boston who wanted to build a summer house, an' he got a heap o' money for it. Anyway, them two loonies ran the farm till one day, Penn's church—the Moravian Christians—found out where he was an' wrote to Uncle Salters. I never heard what they said exactly, but Uncle Salters was mad. He's Episcopalian mostly and he just let 'em have it. He told 'em he wasn't goin' to give up Penn to any Moravian church in Pennsylvania or anywheres else. Then he come to Dad, towin' Penn behind him (that was two trips ago)—an' says he an' Penn must fish a trip for their health. Guess he thought the Moravians wouldn't hunt the Grand Banks for Jacob Boiler. Dad was agreeable, since Uncle Salters had been fishin' off an' on for thirty years. Uncle Salters took a quarter share in the *We're Here*, an' the trip did Penn so much good, Dad made a habit of takin' him. Some day, Dad says, he'll remember his wife an' kids an' Johnstown, an' then, most likely, he'll die, Dad sez. Don't you talk about Johnstown or such things to Penn, or Uncle Salters will heave ye overboard."

"Poor Penn!" murmured Harvey. "I wouldn't have thought Uncle Salters cared for him by the look of 'em together."

"I like Penn, though. We all do," said Dan. "We should've towed him in, but I wanted to tell ye first."

They were close to the schooner now, the

other boats a little behind them.

"Leave the dories till after dinner," said Troop from the deck. "We'll dress down right off. Fix the tables, boys!"

"Deeper'n a whale deep," said Dan, with a wink, as he set the tables. "Look at them boats that have edged up since mornin'. They're all waitin' on Dad. See 'em, Harve?"

"They all look alike to me."

"They ain't, though. That schooner with the two masts, she's called the *Hope of Prague*. Nick Brady's her captain, the meanest man on the Banks. Way off yonder's the *Day's Eye*. The two Jerald brothers own her. She's fast, too, an' has good luck, but Dad could find fish in a graveyard. Them other three, they're the *Margie Smith, Rose,* and *Edith S. Whalen,* all from home. Guess we'll see the *Abbie M. Deering* tomorrow, Dad, won't we?"

"You won't see many boats tomorrow, Danny." When Troop called his son Danny, it was a sign that the old man was pleased. "Boys, we're too crowded," he went on, addressing the crew as they clambered inboard. "We'll leave 'em to bait big an' catch small." He looked at the catch in the pen, and it was curious to see how small the fish were. Except for Harvey's halibut, there was nothing over fifteen pounds on deck.

"I'm waitin' on the weather," he added.

"Looks like fine weather to me, Disko," said

Long Jack, sweeping the clear horizon.

And yet, half an hour later, as they were dressing down the fish, the Grand Banks fog dropped on them. It rolled in steadily, curling and smoking along the colorless water. The men stopped their work without a word. Long Jack and Uncle Salters began to heave up the huge anchor. Manuel and Tom Platt gave a hand and the anchor came up with a thud. Troop steadied the ship at the wheel. "Up jib and foresail," he said.

Long Jack quickly hoisted the "jib"—a small, triangular sail—to the top of the mast at the front of the ship. The others raised the larger "foresail" and the ship creaked as the *We're Here* moved off into the whirling fog.

"There's wind behind this fog," said Troop.

It was wonderful beyond words to Harvey, and the most wonderful part was that he heard no orders except an occasional grunt from Troop, ending with, "That's good, my son!"

"Never seen an anchor raised before?" said Tom Platt, as Harvey stared at the damp canvas of the foresail.

"No. Where are we going?"

"Set sail and fish, as you'll find out 'fore you've been a week aboard. It's all new to you, but we never know what may come to us. Now, take me—Tom Platt—I'd never ha' thought I'd be fishing—"

"It's better than fourteen dollars a month an' a bullet in your belly," said Troop, from the wheel. "Ease your sail a bit."

"The pay's better, sure" returned the Navy man, doing something to a big jib with a wooden pole tied to it. "But we didn't think o' money when we manned the decks of the *Miss Jim Buck*." Tom Platt was referring to a Navy warship. "We was outside Beaufort Harbor in North Carolina. Fort Macon heavin' hot cannon balls at us and a fierce storm on top o' it all. Where was you then, Disko?"

"Right here, or hereabouts," Disko replied, "earnin' my bread on the deep waters. Sorry I can't accommodate you with cannon fire, Tom Platt; but I guess we'll hev a good trip anyways."

There was now a constant commotion of sails slapping and men chattering on deck. This was only broken by the frequent, solid thud of the boat hitting the water, and a spray of water clattering down on deck. The ropes and hooks dripped clammy drops of water. Most of the men lounged along the outermost edge of the deck, where a small ledge sheltered them from the wind. Uncle Salters sat stiffly on the main hatch, nursing his stung hands.

Disko turned the wheel slightly. A few seconds later a hissing wave splashed diagonally across the boat, hit Uncle Salters between the shoulders, and drenched him from head to foot.

He rose and stumbled forward, only to catch another wave.

"Watch Dad chase him all around the deck," said Dan. "Dad's dun this to 'em him two trips runnin'. Ha! That one got 'em good." Uncle Salters had taken shelter by the main mast, but a wave slapped over him. Disko's face was as blank as the circle of the wheel.

"Penn, you go below an' git your coffee!" roared the victim through a cloud of spray. "You ought to hev more sense than to bum around on deck in this weather."

"Now they'll drink coffee an' play checkers till the cows come home," said Dan, as Uncle Salters hustled Penn below deck. "'Looks to me like we'll all be playin' checkers for a spell. Ain't nothin' duller than a fishin' vessel that ain't fishin'.'"

"I'm glad ye spoke, Danny," cried Long Jack, who had been wandering around in search of amusement. "I'd forgot we had a passenger onboard. There's no rest for them that don't know their ropes. Pass him along, Tom Platt, an' we'll teach him."

"Sorry, Harve," grinned Dan. "You've got to go it alone."

For an hour Long Jack walked his prey up and down. He was teaching, as he said, "things at the sea that every man must know, blind, drunk, or asleep." There is not much to see on a seventy-ton schooner, but Long Jack had a talent for

describing things. When he wanted to draw Harvey's attention to the "peak halyards"—the ropes used to hoist the main sail—he dug his knuckles into the back of the boy's neck and made him look up for half a minute. When he wanted to point out the "foreboom"—the long wooden pole that swung out along the bottom of the front sail—he rubbed Harvey's nose along the entire length of it

The lesson would have been easier if the deck wasn't so cluttered. There seemed to be a place for everything and anything, except a man. At the front of the ship was the "windlass"—a large contraption of metal chains, thick cables, and a round drum used to haul up the anchor. Then there was the stove pipe that ran up from the lower decks, and the barrels that held the fish livers. Towards the middle of the ship was the foreboom and the door to the main hatch. These took all the space that was not needed for the dressing pens. Then came the "house"—an enclosed cabin where Disko would steer the ship—and the stacks of dories tied to ring-shaped bolts by the quarterdeck. Finally, there was the sixty-foot main boom tied to the wide bottom of the main sail. The main boom was nearly as long as the ship itself, and the men were constantly ducking and dodging it as they moved about.

Tom Platt, of course, could not keep his oar out of the business. He offered long and unnecessary descriptions of sails and masts on the old *Ohio*.

"Never mind what he says. Listen to me, boy. Tom Platt, this ain't the *Ohio*, an' you're confusin' the boy."

"He'll be ruined for life, beginnin' on a ship like this," Tom Platt pleaded. "Give him a chance to know a few leadin' principles. Sailing's an art, Harvey, as I'd show you if I had ye in the 'ol *Ohio* . . ."

"Ye'd talk him to death. Silence, Tom Platt!

Now, after all I've said, how do you roll up the foresail, Harve? Take your time answerin'."

"Haul that in," said Harvey, pointing into the wind.

"What? The North Atlantic?"

"No, the boom. Then run that rope you showed me back there—"

"That's no way," Tom Platt burst in.

"Quiet! He's learnin', an' does not know the names good yet. Go on, Harve."

"Oh, it's the reef pennant. I'd hook the tackle on to the reef pennant, and then let down—"

"Lower the sail, child! Lower!" said Tom Platt, in agony.

"Lower the throat and peak halyards," Harvey went on. Those names stuck in his head.

"Lay your hand on them," said Long Jack.

Harvey obeyed. "Lower till that rope loop—the cringle—was down on the boom. Then I'd tie her up the way you said, and then I'd hoist up the peak and throat halyards again."

"You've forgot to pass the tackle, but with time and help ye'll learn. There's a good reason for every rope aboard, or else ye would be overboard. Understand? 'Tis dollars an' cents I'm puttin' into your pocket, ye skinny little cargo. Ye can sail from Boston to Cuba and tell 'em Long Jack taught you. Now I'll chase ye around a bit, callin' the ropes, an' you'll lay your hand on them as I call."

He began, and Harvey, who was feeling rather tired, walked slowly to the rope named. Then the ragged end of a rope whipped round his ribs and nearly knocked the breath out of him.

"When you own a boat, you can walk," said Tom Platt, with serious eyes. "Till then, when you get an order, you run. Once more—to make sure!"

Harvey was already annoyed at Long Jack's game, and this last cut angered him even more. But Harvey was a smart boy. He looked at the other men, and saw that even Dan did not smile. Apparently, this was all in the day's work, so he took the hint with a gulp and a gasp and a grin. The same smartness that led him to take such advantage of his mother made him very sure that no one on the boat (except, maybe, Penn) would stand the least bit of nonsense from him. Long Jack called out the names of a half dozen ropes, and Harvey danced around the deck like an eel at low tide. He kept an eye on Tom Platt the whole time.

"Very good. Very good," said Manuel. "After supper I show you a little schooner I make, with all her ropes. We shall learn."

"First-class for—a passenger," said Dan. "Dad sez ye may be worth your salt before you're drowned. That's sayin' a heap fer Dad. I'll teach ye more durin' our next watch together."

"Lead!" grunted Disko, peering through the fog as it smoked over the bows. There was nothing to be seen ten feet beyond the ship. Alongside, an endless procession of sad, pale waves whispered by.

"Now I'll teach you something Long Jack can't," shouted Tom Platt. He emerged from a locker with a battered "lead"—a fishing line with a weight on the end that was used to measure water depth.

Disko did something to the wheel that slowed the boat. Manuel let down the jib with Harvey's help (and Harvey was a very proud boy). Then Tom Platt released the lead, which plopped into the sea.

"This is important," said Dan. "When your thick in fog, a lead's the only eyes you hev. What d'you make it, Dad?"

Disko's face relaxed. He had a reputation as a master artist who knew the Banks blindfolded. "Sixty feet, mebbe—if I'm any judge," he replied, with a glance at the tiny compass in the window of the "house."

"Sixty," announced Tom Platt, hauling in the line.

The schooner gained speed once more. "Lead!" said Disko, after fifteen minutes.

"What d'you make it?" Dan whispered, and he looked at Harvey proudly. But Harvey was too proud of his own performances to be impressed just then.

"Fifty," said the father. "I suspect we're right

over the Green Bank."

"Fifty!" roared Tom Platt. They could scarcely see him through the fog.

"Bait up, Harve," said Dan, diving for a fishing line.

The schooner seemed to be straying randomly through the fog. Her sails banged wildly. The men waited and looked at the boys, who began fishing.

"Ha!" Dan's lines twitched on the rail. "Now how in thunder did Dad know? Help us here, Harve. It's a big one." They hauled together, and landed a twenty pound cod. He had taken the bait right into his stomach.

"Why, he's all covered with little crabs," cried Harvey, turning him over.

"By God," said Long Jack. "Disko, I swear ye keep your spare eyes under the boat."

Splash went the anchor, and they all heaved over the fishing lines, each man taking his own place at the sides of the ship.

"Are they good to eat?" Harvey panted, as he lugged in another crab-covered cod.

"Sure. The crabs mean they've all been herdin' together by the thousand, right down to bottom. An' when they take the bait that way they're hungry. Never mind how the bait sets. They'll bite on the bare hook."

"Say, this is great!" Harvey cried, as the fish came in gasping and splashing. "Why can't we always fish from the boat instead of from the dories?"

"We can, till we start to clean 'em. After that, the heads and backbones will scare off the fish. Boatfishin' ain't consider'd modern, though. Guess we'll set out some trawl tonight. That's fishin' line with a bunch o' hooks hangin' off it, Harve. Harder on the back than from the dory, ain't it?"

It was rather back-breaking work. The schooner was much higher than a dory, so the fish had to be hauled up much further. But it was a wild and furious sport as long as it lasted, and a big pile lay aboard when the fish stopped biting.

"Where's Penn and Uncle Salters?" Harvey asked, slapping the slime off his oilskins, and reeling up the line in careful imitation of the others.

"Git some coffee and see."

Below deck, under the yellow glare of a lamp, sat Uncle Salters and Penn, with a checker board between them. The men were completely unaware of the fish or the weather.

"What's the matter now?" said Uncle Salters.

"Big fish—heaps and heaps," Harvey replied. "How's the game?"

Little Penn's jaw dropped. "Fish!? Well, it wasn't none o' his fault that we didn't come up," snapped Uncle Salters. "Penn's deaf."

"Checkers?" said Dan, as Harvey staggered back with the steaming coffee in a tin pail. "That gits us out of cleanin' up tonight. Dad's a fair man. They'll have to do it."

"An' two young fellers I know will bait up the trawl while they're cleanin'," said Disko, securing a rope to the wheel to hold it steady.

"Um, guess I'd 'ruther clean up, Dad."

"Don't doubt it. Ye won't, though. Dress down! Dress down! Penn'll pitch while you two set bait on the trawl."

"Why in thunder didn't them boys tell us you'd struck fish?" said Uncle Salters, shuffling to his place at the table. "This knife ain't sharp, Dan."

Dan bent over the tubs full of trawl line. "Hey, Harve, why don't ye slip down below an' git us bait?"

"Bait as we are," said Disko.

That meant the boys would use selected bits of cod as the fish were cleaned. This was far better than shoving bare hands into the little bait barrels below. The trawl tubs were full of neatly coiled line with a big hook every few feet. Each hook must be baited and checked. Then the lines must be packed with scientific care, so they don't tangle when thrown from the dories. Dan managed it in the dark, without looking, while Harvey constantly caught his fingers on the hooks.

"I helped bait trawl before I could walk," he said. "But it's a dull job all the same. Oh, Dad!" This was shouted towards the hatch, where Disko and Tom Platt were salting down below. "How many you reckon we'll need?"

"'Bout three. Hurry!"

"There's three hundred fathom o' line to each tub," Dan explained. "More'n enough to lay out tonight. Ouch! Slipped up there, I did." He stuck his finger in his mouth. "I tell you, Harve, there ain't enough money in Gloucester to hire me to ship on a reg'lar trawler. It may be consider'd the modern way o' doing things, but it's the dullest business on earth."

"My fingers are cut to pieces," Harvey sulked.

"This is just one o' Dad's experiments. He don't trawl unless there's mighty good reason fer it. Dad knows. We'll hev her saggin' full o' fish."

Penn and Uncle Salters cleaned up as Disko had ordered, but this didn't get the boys out of more work themselves. No sooner were the tubs finished than Tom Platt and Long Jack, who had been exploring the inside of a dory with a lantern, snatched them away. They loaded up the tubs and some small, painted trawl buoys that would float at the surface once the lines had been cast. The men then heaved the boat overboard into what Harvey considered very rough sea. "They'll be drowned. Why, the dory's loaded like a freight train," he cried.

"We'll be back," said Long Jack, "an' we'll lay into ye both if the trawl gits tangled."

The dory surged up on the crest of a wave, and just when it seemed impossible that she could avoid smashing against the schooner's side, slid over the ridge, and disappeared in the damp dusk.

"Take this, an' keep it ringin'," said Dan, passing Harvey a bell.

Harvey rang vigorously, for he felt two lives depended on him. But Disko did not look like a murderer, and when he went to supper he even smiled at the anxious Harvey.

"This ain't no weather to worry 'bout," said Dan. "Why, you an' me could set the trawl! They don't need no bell really."

"Clang! clang! clang!" Harvey kept it up for another half hour. There was a holler and a bump alongside. Manuel and Dan raced to the men and hoisted the boat. Long Jack and Tom Platt arrived on deck together, and the dory followed them in the air, landing with a clatter.

"Not one tangle," said Tom Platt as he dripped. "Danny, ye did good."

"The pleasure uv your comp'ny to the banquet," said Long Jack, shaking the water from his boots and sticking an oil-skinned arm into Harvey's face. "We'll be honorin' the second half wit our presence." The four men went off to supper, where Harvey stuffed himself to the brim on fish chowder and fried pies. He then fell fast asleep, just as Manuel arrived with a lovely two-foot model of a schooner to show Harvey the ropes. Harvey never even moved a finger as Penn pushed him into his bunk.

"It must be a sad thing—a very sad thing," said Penn, watching the boy's face, "for his mother and his father, who think he is dead. To lose a child—to lose a young man!"

"Change the subject, Penn," said Dan. "Go finish your game with Uncle Salters. Tell Dad I'll stand Harve's watch if he don't care. He's worn out."

"Ver' good boy," said Manuel, slipping out of his boots and disappearing into the black shadows of the lower bunk. "Expec' he'll make a good man, Danny. I don't thinks he's as crazy as your papa sez."

Dan smiled, but the smile ended in a snore.

The fog was thick outside, and the wind was gaining strength. The older men stood watch in shifts, as the ship slapped and scraped against the sea. The hot stovepipe hissed as the sea spray splashed against it. The boys slept on while Disko, Long Jack, Tom Platt, and Uncle Salters took turns at the wheel, making sure the anchor held, and glancing at the dim anchor light between each round.

CHAPTER 4

Harvey awoke in his bunk to find the "first half" eating breakfast at the table. The door to the upper deck was open a crack, and every square inch of the schooner was alive with noise and motion. The cook balanced in his tiny workspace behind the wood-burning stove. The pots and pans clanged loudly as they swung from hooks overhead. Up and up the ship would climb, then pause for a moment before plunging down again into the seas. Harvey could hear the water splashing over the deck above, and the grunts and creaks of the ship as she gathered herself together to repeat the motions.

"Now, if we were ashore," he heard Long Jack saying, "we'd hev chores to do in any weather. Here, we've no chores at all. That's a blessin'. Good night, all." He moved like a big snake from the table to his bunk, and began to smoke. Tom Platt followed his example. Uncle Salters, with Penn, fought his way up the ladder to stand his watch, and the cook set the table for the "second half."

The "second half" came out of its bunks with a stretch and a yawn. They ate till they could eat no more. Then Manuel filled his pipe with some terrible tobacco, kicked his feet up on the table, and smiled tender smiles at the smoke. Dan stretched out in his bunk, wrestling with a gaudy, gold-colored accordion, whose melody went up and down with the rocking of the *We're Here*. The cook, his shoulders against the locker where he kept the fried pies (Dan was fond of fried pies), peeled potatoes. He kept one eye on the stove in case too much sea water splashed its way down the pipe.

The smell and smoke were beyond description, and Harvey was amazed he was not deathly sick. He crawled back into his bunk, the softest and safest place he could find, while Dan tried his best to play a tune amid the ship's wild jerking.

"How long is this for?" Harvey asked of Manuel.

"Till she get a little quiet, and we can row to the trawl. Perhaps tonight. Perhaps two days more. You do not like?"

"I would have been crazy sick a week ago, but it doesn't seem to bother me now—much."

"That is because we make you fisherman. If I was you, when I come to Gloucester I would give two, three big candles for my good luck."

"Give who?"

"To the Virgin of our Church on the Hill.

She is very good to fishermen all the time. That is why so few of us Portuguese men ever are drowned. I always give candles—two, three or more when I come to Gloucester. The good Virgin, she never forgets me, Manuel."

"I don't sense it that way," said Tom Platt from his bunk, his scarred face lit up by the glare of a match as he sucked at his pipe. "The sea's the sea, simple as that, and you'll get jest about whatever she wants to give ye, candles or not."

"'Tis a mighty good thing," said Long Jack, "to have a friend upstairs, though. I agree with Manuel. About ten years back I was workin' a South Boston boat when a fierce storm come down on us. The captain was drunk, his chin waggin' on the floor, an' I sez to myself, 'If I ever make it back to shore, I'll show the saints exactly what kind o' ship they saved me out of.' Now I'm still here, as ye can see, an' the model of the dirty ol' ship, that took me a month to make, I gave it to the priest. He hung it up right next to the altar. There's more sense in givin' a model. It's a work of art. Ye can buy candles at any store, but a model shows the good saints ye've gone to some trouble an' are grateful."

"D'you really believe that, Irish?" said Tom Platt, turning on his elbow.

"Would I do it if I did not, Ohio?"

"Well, Jim Fuller, he made a model o' the old *Ohio,* and it's in the Salem museum now. Mighty pretty model, too, but he weren't much o' a sailor anyways. I remember . . ."

The discussion went on like this for an hour. The men shouted and talked in circles, and no one proved anything at the end. But it was clear the fishermen were enjoying themselves, and would have continued if Dan hadn't started to play a cheerful song:

**Up jumped the mackerel with his stripe'd
back.
Lower the mainsail, and haul on the tack;
For it's windy weather—"
Here Long Jack joined in:
And it's blowy weather;
When the winds begin to blow,
all hands together!**

Dan went on, with a cautious look at Tom Platt, holding the accordion low in the bunk.
Tom Platt seemed to be hunting for something.
Dan crouched lower, but sang louder:

"Up jumped the flounder that swims to the ground . . ."

Tom Platt's huge rubber boot flew across the room and caught Dan's uplifted arm. There was war between the man and the boy ever since Dan had discovered that the mere whistling of that song would make him angry.

Dan threw the boot back with precision. "Ef you don't like my music, git out your fiddle. I ain't goin' to lie here all day an' listen to you an'

Long Jack arguin' 'bout candles. Fiddle, Tom Platt, or I'll teach Harve here the song!"

Tom Platt leaned down to a locker and brought up an old white fiddle. Manuel's eye glistened, and from somewhere behind him, drew out a tiny, guitar-like thing with wire strings, which he called a machette.

"'Tis a concert," said Long Jack, beaming through the smoke. "A reg'lar Boston concert."

There was a burst of spray as the hatch opened, and Disko, in yellow oilskins, descended.

"Ye're just in time, Disko. What's she doin' outside?"

"Just this!" He stumbled into the ladder as the *We're Here* rolled to one side.

"We're singin' to keep our breakfasts down. Ye'll lead us in a song, of course, Disko," said Long Jack.

"I don't know more'n two old songs, an' ye've heard 'em both."

His excuses were cut short by Tom Platt launching into a most sorrowful tune. It sounded like the moaning of winds and the creaking of masts. Then, with his eyes fixed on the wooden beams above, Disko began an ancient song about an old schooner that sailed the Grand Banks. There were scores of verses. He described every mile of the fabled ship called the "Dreadnought" for every mile of its journey from Liverpool, England and New York as if he were on her deck.

All the while, the accordion pumped and the fiddle squeaked beside him.

Tom Platt followed with something about "the rough and tough McGinn, who would pilot the vessel in." Then Manuel took up his little machette and sang something in Portuguese about "Nina, innocente!" He ended the strange melody with a dramatic sweep of his hand. Then Disko obliged with his second song, and all joined in to sing along:

Now April is over and melted the snow,
And out of New Bedford we shortly must tow;
Yes, out o' New Bedford we shortly must clear,
We're the whalers that never see wheat in the ear."

Harvey thought about the whalers who went to sea every spring, and never get to see the wheat fields grow high enough to tickle your ears. This almost made Harvey cry, though he could not tell why. But it was much worse when the cook dropped the potatoes and held out his hands for the fiddle. Still leaning against the locker door, he played a strange and haunting melody. After a while he sang, in an unknown language, his big chin down on the fiddle, his white eyeballs shining in the lamplight. Harvey swung out of his bunk to hear better; and amid the creaking of the ship and the wash of the waters, the cook wailed through the song.

"Jimmy Christmas! That one gives me the

creeps," said Dan. "What in thunder is it?"

"The song of Fin McCoul," said the cook, "when he was going to Norway." His English was very clear.

"I've been to Norway, but I didn't make that awful noise. 'Tis like some of the old mariner songs, though," said Long Jack, sighing.

"Don't let's hev another without somethin' between," said Dan; and the accordion struck up a catchy tune that ended:

"It's six an' twenty Sundays since last we saw the land,

With fifteen thousand pounds,

And fifteen thousand pounds,

And fifteen thousand pounds,

'Tween old Gloucester an' Grand!"

"Hold on!" roared Tom Platt. "D'ye want to curse the trip, Dan? That's Jonah for sure!"

"No it ain't, is it, Dad? Not unless you sing the very las' verse. You can't tell me anything on Jonahs!"

"What's that?" said Harvey. "What's a Jonah?"

"A Jonah's anything that spoils good luck. Sometimes it's a man—sometimes it's a boy—or a bucket," said Tom Platt. "There's all sorts o' Jonahs. Jim Bourke was one till he was drowned. I'd never ship with Jim Bourke, not if I was starvin'. There wuz a green dory on a ship I once worked. That was a Jonah, too, the worst sort o'

Jonah. Drowned four men, she did."

"And you believe that?" said Harvey, remembering what Tom Platt had said about candles. "Isn't that just superstition?"

A mutter of disagreement ran round the bunks. "On shore, yes. At sea, anything can happen," said Disko. "Don't you go makin' fun of Jonahs, young feller."

"Well, Harve ain't no Jonah. Day after we found him," Dan cut in, "we had a toppin' good catch."

The cook threw up his head and laughed suddenly.

"What's wrong?" said Dan. "Ain't he our mascot? And didn't they fish good after we fished up Harve?"

"Oh! yes," said the cook. "I know that, but the catch is not finish yet."

"He ain't goin' to do us any harm," said Dan, hotly. "What are ye hintin' at? He's all right"

"No harm. No. But one day he will be your master, Danny."

"Is that all?" said Dan calmly. "He won't."

"Master!" said the cook, pointing to Harvey. "Man!" and he pointed to Dan.

"That's news. How soon?" said Dan, with a laugh.

"In some years, and I shall see it. Master and man—man and master."

"How in thunder d'ye work that out?" said

Tom Platt.

"In my head, where I can see."

"How?"

"I do not know, but I am right." He dropped his head, and went on peeling the potatoes. He would not say another word.

"Well," said Dan, "a heap o' things'll hev to happen before Harve's any master o' mine. But I'm glad the doctor ain't choosin' to call him a Jonah. Now, I suspect Uncle Salters is the Jonerest Jonah in the entire fleet. He ought to be on the *Carrie Pitman*. That boat's her own Jonah, fer sure."

"We're well clear o' the fleet anyway," said Disko. "*Carrie Pitman* and every other ship." There was a knocking on the deck.

"Uncle Salters finally brought us some luck," said Dan as his father departed.

"Weather's clear," Disko cried, and all the men tumbled up for a bit of fresh air. The fog had gone, but the sea ran in great long waves behind it. The *We're Here* slid up and down on the water, which shifted and rose without rest.

"Seems to me I saw somethin' flicker jest now over yonder," said Uncle Salters, pointing to the northeast.

"Can't be any of the fleet," said Disko, peering under his eyebrows. "Sea's calmin' down fast. Danny, don't you want to skip up a piece an' see how our trawl buoy lays?"

Danny, in his big boots, trotted rather than climbed up the main mast (this consumed Harvey with jealousy), and hitched himself around the "crosstrees" or wooden poles that ran horizontally from the top of the masts. Dan let his eye roam till it caught the tiny black buoy flag on the top of a wave a mile away.

"She's all right," he hailed. Then he spotted the other ship. "Sail-O! Dead to the north! She's a schooner, too."

They waited yet another half hour, the sky clearing in patches, with a flicker of sun from time to time. Then they spotted a foremast in the distance.

"Frenchmen!" shouted Dan. "No, it ain't. Da-a-aaad!"

"That's no French ship," said Disko. "Salters, your bad luck holds tighter'n a screw."

"I've got eyes. It's Uncle Abishal."

"The king of all Jonahs," groaned Tom Platt. "Oh, Salters, Salters, why wasn't you in bed an' asleep?"

It was a tattered, foul and messy ship that seemed to barely keep its balance. Her ropes flew loosely in the rough sea and tangled together like weeds. Her booms had been patched and nailed beyond further repair. She drifted and veered around awkwardly, lifting up and sitting back down on her wide backside with each new wave. Next to the *We're Here*, she looked like a nasty old woman sneering at a decent girl.

"That's Abishal," said Salters. "Full o' gin and wild men."

"Ain't she low in the front more 'n natural, Tom Platt?," said Disko.

"If she's split her seams and takin' on water, he better git to his pumps mighty quick," said the sailor slowly.

The schooner was now within earshot. A gray beard wagged over the side of the schooner, and a thick voice yelled something Harvey could not understand. But Disko's face darkened. "He'd risk every sail he has to carry bad news. Says we're in fer bad weather. He's in fer worse, though. Abishal! Abi-shal!" He waved his arm up and down with the gesture of a man at the water pumps, and pointed to the front of their boat. The crew mocked him and laughed.

"A livin' storm! A livin' storm!" yelled Uncle Abishal. "Prepare fer ye last trip, all you Gloucester fish. You won't see Gloucester no more, no more!"

"Crazy drunk—as usual," said Tom Platt. "Wish he hadn't seen us, though."

She drifted out of hearing while the gray beard yelled something about a dead man in the lower cabin. Harvey trembled. He had seen the filthy decks and the savage-eyed crew.

"Now there's a fine floatin' hell fer ye," said Long Jack. "I wonder what trouble he's been into on shore."

"He's a trawler," Dan explained to Harvey, "an' he runs ashore for bait all along the coast. He deals along the south an' east shore up yonder." He nodded in the direction of the Newfoundland beaches. "Dad won't never take me ashore there. They're a mighty tough crowd—an' Abishal's the toughest. You saw his boat? Well, she's seventy year old, they say; the last o' her kind. She was made in Boston, but Abishal don't go to Boston no more. He ain't wanted there. He just drifts around the Banks, in debt, trawlin' an' cussin' like you heard. Been a

Jonah fer years an' years, he has. Crazy, I guess."

The beat-up boat danced drunkenly away, and all eyes followed her. Suddenly the cook cried: "It was his own death that made him speak so! Look!" The boat sailed into a patch of watery sunshine three or four miles away. Then she dipped below the horizon, and disappeared.

"Turn about!" shouted Disko. "Drunk or sober, we've got to help 'em. Heave up the anchor! Go!"

Harvey was thrown on the deck by the shock that followed the raising of the jib and foresail. The men yanked on the cables, and to save time, jerked up the anchor by hand. This sort of brute force is only used in matters of life and death. They sailed down to where Abishal's craft had vanished and found two or three barrels and a gin bottle, but nothing more.

"Let 'em go," said Disko, though no one had hinted at picking them up. "I wouldn't hev a match that belonged to Abishal aboard. Guess she ran clear into the sea. Must've split her seams and been leakin' fer a week. Bet they never thought to pump out the water. That's one more boat that sunk thanks to leavin' port with a drunken crew."

"Glory be!" said Long Jack. "We'd ha' been obliged to help 'em if they was on top o' the water."

"'Thinkin' o' that myself," said Tom Platt.

"He has taken his bad luck with him," said the cook.

Penn sat down and sobbed at the sheer horror and pity of it all. Harvey did not realize that he had seen death on the open waters, but he felt very sick. Then Dan scrambled up the crosstrees, and Disko steered them back to within sight of their own trawl buoys just before the fog blanketed the sea once again.

"At sea, when we go, we go mighty quick," was all he said to Harvey. "You think about that fer a spell, young feller. That was caused by liquor."

After dinner it was calm enough to fish from the decks, and the catch was huge with large fish.

"Abishal has surely took his bad luck with him," said Salters. "The wind ain't kicked up at all. How about the trawl? I don't like superstition anyway."

Tom Platt insisted that they were better off hauling in the trawl and finding a new place to lay anchor. But the cook said: "The line is cut in two pieces. You will find it so when you look. I know." This so excited Long Jack that he took Tom Platt by the arm and the two went out together.

"Underrunning" a trawl means pulling it in on one side of the dory, picking off the fish, rebaiting the hooks, and passing them back to the sea again. It was something like pinning and unpinning clothes on a wash line. It is a time-consuming task and rather dangerous, for the long, sagging line can pull a boat under in an instant. But when they heard, "And now to thee, O Captain," booming out of the fog, the crew of the *We're Here* smiled. The dory swirled along-side, well loaded with fish. Tom Platt yelled for Manuel to act as relief boat.

"The line's cut square in two pieces," said Long Jack, forking in the fish. "One half was just pumpkins. Tom Platt wanted to haul her in an' have done wid it. But I said, "I'll back the doctor that has the second sight. That man can see the future. Then, sure enough, the other half come up sagging full o' big fish. Hurry, Manuel, an' bring a tub o' bait. There's luck afloat tonight."

The fish bit at the newly baited hooks, and Tom Platt and Long Jack moved methodically up and down the length of the trawl, stripping the type of jellyfish they called pumpkins, rebaiting, and loading Manuel's dory till dusk.

"I'll take no risks with our luck," said Disko then, "not with him floatin' around so near. Abishal won't sink fer a week. Heave in the dories an' we'll dress down after supper."

It was a long dressing-down that lasted till nine o'clock. Disko was heard chuckling from time to time as Harvey pitched the fish down below.

"Say, you were pitchin' awful fast tonight," said Dan, as they sharpened the knives after the men had turned in. "There's somethin' of a rough sea tonight, an' I ain't heard you make no complaints about it."

"Too busy," Harvey replied, testing a blade's edge. "Come to think of it, the ship sure is kicking, isn't she?"

The little schooner was skipping all around her anchor among the silver-tipped waves. She fidgeted and wriggled on the anchor rope, like a puppy chewing a string, or a cow stung by a hornet.

"She sure is sayin' her piece. She's like Patrick Henry. Give me liberty or give me death!" said Dan.

She swung sideways on a wave, and swept her jib boom across the deck. Then, wop! She sat down on the water.

Harvey laughed aloud. "Why, it's just as if she was alive," he said.

"She's as sturdy as a house," said Dan enthusiastically, as he was swept across the deck in a batter of spray. "She fends 'em off an' fends 'em off, an' says 'Don't ye come near me.' Look at her—jest look at her! You should see one o' them toothpicks hoistin' up her anchor."

"What's a toothpick, Dan?"

"Them new boats that fish for haddock an' herring. Fine as a yacht, they are. Dad's set against 'em on account o' how they roll and jolt around in the water, but there's heaps o' money in 'em. Dad can find fish, but he ain't no ways progressive. He don't go with the march o' the times. Those toothpicks are chockfull o' time-savin' tools an' everything."

"What do they cost, Dan?"

"Hills o' dollars. Fifteen thousand, perhaps. More, mebbe. They hev everything you kin think of." Then to himself, half under his breath, "Guess I'd call her *Hattie S.*, too."

CHAPTER 5

That was the first of many talks with Dan, who told Harvey why he would transfer his dory's name to the imaginary "toothpick" ship. Harvey heard a good deal about the real Hattie from Gloucester, Massachusetts. He even saw a lock of her hair—which Dan had stolen as she sat in front of him at school that winter—and a photograph. Hattie was about fourteen years old, with an awful dislike for boys, and had been trampling on Dan's heart through the winter. All this was revealed under an oath of secrecy on moonlit decks, in the dead dark, or in thick fog. Once, of course, as the boys came to know each other, there was a fight, which raged from one end of the deck to the other. Penn finally separated them, but promised not to tell Disko, who thought that fighting on watch was worse than sleeping. Harvey was no match for Dan physically, but it says a great deal for his new training that he accepted his defeat and did not try to get even with Dan by underhanded methods.

That was after Harvey had been cured of a string of blisters between his elbows and wrists, where the wet jersey and oilskins cut into the flesh. The salt water stung them terribly, but when the blisters had opened, Dan cleaned them out with Disko's razor, and assured Harvey that now he was a true member of the crew.

Since he was a boy and very busy, he did not bother his head with too much thinking. He was extremely sorry for his mother, and often longed to see her and above all to tell her of this wonderful new life, and how he was doing so well in it. Otherwise, he preferred not to wonder too much how she was coping with his supposed death. But one day, as he stood on the ladder to the lower deck, arguing with the cook, who had accused him and Dan of sneaking fried pies, it occurred to him that this was a vast improvement over being ignored by strangers in the smoking room of a passenger ship.

He was part of the team on the *We're Here*. He had his place at the table and among the bunks, and could hold his own in the long talks on stormy days, when the others were always ready to listen to what they called his "fairy tales" of his life ashore. It did not take him more than two days to feel that if he spoke about his own life—it seemed very far away—no one except Dan believed him (and even Dan's belief was sorely tried). So he invented a friend, a boy he had heard of, who drove a miniature four-pony carriage in Toledo, Ohio, and ordered five suits of clothes at a time and held parties where the oldest girl was not quite fifteen, but all the presents were solid silver. Salters protested that this kind of talk was desperately wicked, if not positively blasphemous, but he listened as greedily as the others. In the end, their criticisms gave Harvey entirely new opinions of clothes, rings, watches, small dinner parties, champagne, card-playing, and hotel accommodation. Little by little he changed his tone when speaking of his "friend," whom Long Jack had christened "the Crazy Kid," "the Gold-Plated Baby," and other pet names. Harvey was a very adaptable person, with a keen eye and ear for every face and tone of voice about him.

Before long he knew where Disko kept what that they called the "hog yoke." It was an arc-shaped instrument that measured the distance of the stars and the location of the sun. Disko used the hog yoke, along with the *Old Farmer's Almanac,* to calculate the ship's latitude and longitude. Each time Disko took these measurements, Harvey would jump down into the cabin and scratch the location and date with a nail on the rusty stovepipe. Harvey performed this task with the seriousness of a chief engineer. He felt it was extremely important to post the schooner's location for that day. After he had done this—and

not until then—would he carefully return the hog yoke to the bag beneath Disko's bunk.

The hog yoke, the *Eldridge Tide and Pilot Book*, the *Farmers Almanac*, and a pair of other books named *Coast Pilot*, and *Navigator*, were all the weapons Disko needed to guide the *We're Here*. And he always had his spare eye: the deep-sea lead that measured the depth of the water. Harvey nearly killed Penn with it when Tom Platt first taught him how to "sound," as the men would call it. Harvey was not strong enough to haul up the heavier weights the men used in rough seas. But when the water was calm, Disko used him freely.

Not only did the lead measure water depth, it also provided a sample of the sea floor, thanks to a small cup attached to the weight. As Dan said: "'T'ain't soundin's dad wants. It's samples. Grease her up good, Harve." Harvey would slather the cup with sticky fat before plopping it into the water. Then he would carefully bring the sand, shell, sludge, or whatever it collected, to Disko, who fingered and smelled it and gave his judgments. It was said that when Disko thought about cod, he thought as if he was a cod. With some mysterious mixture of instinct and experience, he moved the *We're Here* from place to place, and always found fish. He was like a blindfolded chess player making careful moves on the unseen board. But Disko's board was the Grand Bank—a triangle two hundred and fifty miles on each side. It was a vast expanse of surging seas, thick fog, fierce storms and drifting ice.

They worked in the fog for days. Harvey stayed behind to man the bell, until he was used to the thick fog and finally went out in a dory with Tom Platt. Harvey was terribly nervous, but the fog would not lift and the fish were biting, and no one can stay helplessly afraid for six hours at a time. Harvey tried his best to concentrate on his fishing lines and ignore his fear. Much to his surprise, it was a magical experience, and for the first time that night, Harvey dreamed of the shifting, smoking floors of water around the dory, the fishing lines that strayed away into nothing, and the air above that melted on the sea below.

A few days later he was out with Manuel. The water should have been about forty fathoms deep, but the anchor ran its entire length of rope and did not hit the bottom. Harvey grew mortally afraid that he would never touch the earth again.

"We're in de whale hole," said Manuel, hauling in the anchor. "That is good joke on Disko. Come!" Manuel rowed to the schooner to find Tom Platt and the others already teasing their captain. For the first time, he had led them to the edge of the "whale hole," an enormous, empty crater in the Grand Banks. They sailed forward through the fog to find a better location, and when he went out in Manuel's dory, the hair on Harvey's head stood up in terror. Something large and white, and deathly cold, moved towards them through the fog. Harvey heard a roaring sound, and something tumble down and hit the water. It was his first introduction to the dreaded summer icebergs of the Banks, and he trembled in the bottom of the boat while Manuel laughed.

But there were other days when the weather was clear and warm. It seemed like a sin to do anything but lay on the decks and watch the sun move across the water. And there were days when the sea was perfectly calm, and Harvey was taught how to steer the schooner from one fishing spot to another.

Harvey was very proud when he first turned the steering wheel and felt the ship respond to his command. It was a magnificent moment. But, as usual, his pride was short-lived. To show Dan how completely he had mastered the art of sailing, Harvey made a sharp turn into the wind, then watched in horror as the mast flew across the deck and ripped right through a sail. They lowered the wreck in awful silence, and for the next few days, Harvey spent his leisure hours learning how to use a needle and thread. Dan hollered with joy since, as he said, he had made the very same mistake himself in his early days.

Harvey imitated all the men in turns. He copied the peculiar way Disko stooped at the wheel, and Long Jack's overhanded reach when the fishing lines were hauled in. He studied Manuel's skillful stroke in a dory, and Tom Platt's confident stride on the deck.

"'Tis beautiful to see how he takes to ut," said Long Jack, when Harvey was looking out at the ocean one foggy afternoon. "I'll bet my salary he's more'n half play-acting, and he's convinced himself he's a true mariner. Look at the lil' bit of muscle on his back now!"

"That's the way we all begin," said Tom Platt. "The boys, they make believe all the time till they've pretended 'emselves into bein' men. I done it on the old *Ohio*, I know. Dan's full o' the same kind o' notions. See 'em now, actin' like genuine mariners, as they should." He spoke down the cabin stairs. "Guess you're mistook in your judgments fer once, Disko. What made ye tell us the kid was crazy?"

"He wuz," Disko replied. "Crazy as a loon when he come aboard, but I'll say he's sobered up since. I cured him."

"He sure is entertainin'," said Tom Platt. "The other night he told us about a kid of his own age, steerin' a fancy little wagon an' four ponies up an' down Toledo, Ohio. Curious kind o' fairy tale, but interestin' nonetheless. He knows scores of 'em."

"Guess he makes 'em up in his own head," Disko called from the cabin. He was concentrating on the pages of his logbook, where he made careful entries each day. This was the kind of thing that was written on page after soiled page:

"July 17. This day thick fog and few fish. Sailed northward. So ends this day.

"July 18. This day comes in with thick fog. Caught a few fish.

"July 19. This day comes in with light breeze from Northeast and fine weather. Made a turn eastward. Caught plenty fish.

"July 20. This, the Sabbath, comes in with fog and light winds. So ends this day. Total fish caught this week, 3,478."

They never worked on Sundays, but shaved and washed themselves while Pennsylvania sang church hymns. Once or twice he suggested that perhaps he could preach a little. Uncle Salters nearly jumped down his throat at the mere notion, reminding him that he was not a preacher and mustn't think of such things. "We'd hev him rememberin' Johnstown next," Salters explained, "an' what would happen then?" So they compromised on his reading aloud from a book called *Josephus*. It was an old leather-bound volume that smelled like a hundred sea voyages. It was very thick and very like the Bible, but filled with accounts of battles and attacks; and they read it nearly from cover to cover. Otherwise Penn was a silent little body. He would not utter a word for three days on end sometimes, though he played checkers, listened to the songs, and laughed at the stories. When they tried to talk to him, he would answer: "I don't wish to seem unneighbourly, but it is because I have nothing to say. My head feels quite empty. I've almost forgotten my name." He would turn to Uncle Salters with a nervous smile.

"Why, Pennsylvania Pratt," Salters would shout. "You'll fergit me next!"

"No—never," Penn would say, shutting his lips firmly. "My name is Pennsylvania Pratt, of course," he would repeat over and over.

He was always very tender with Harvey,

whom he pitied both as a lost child and as a lunatic. When Salters saw that Penn liked the boy, he relaxed, too. Salters was not a friendly person, and he considered it his business to keep the boys in line. The first time Harvey managed to climb the main mast, he considered it his business to hang Salters' big sea boots up there—a sign of shame and ridicule to the nearest schooner. Harvey would never play such a joke on Disko, not even when the old man hollered direct orders or spoke to him (like he did to the rest of the crew). "Don't you want to do so and so?" and "Guess you'd better," and so forth. There was something about Disko's clean-shaven lips and wrinkled corners of the eyes that was very intimidating to young blood.

Disko showed Harvey how to use the charts and maps. He led him, pencil in hand, over the whole string of banks that spanned the North Atlantic. He also explained the science behind the "hog yoke," which Harvey excelled at immediately. The idea of stealing information from one glimpse at the sun appealed to Harvey's sharp mind. But when it came to other matters of the sea, Harvey's age worked against him. As Disko said, he should have started when he was ten. Dan could bait up trawl or lay his hand on any rope in the dark. When Uncle Salters had a sting on his hand, Dan could dress down the fish with his eyes closed. He could steer in almost any kind of weather simply from the feel of the wind on his face. He did these things as automatically as he scooted up the main mast, or rowed his dory like it was part of his own body. But he could not communicate his knowledge to Harvey.

Still there was a good deal of general information flying about the schooner on stormy days, when the men took shelter below deck. Disko spoke of whaling voyages from years ago, of great she-whales slaughtered beside their young, and blood that spurted forty feet in the air; of boats smashed to splinters, and the terrible winter of 1871, when twelve hundred men were made homeless on the ice in three days. They were wonderful tales, and all true. But more wonderful were his stories of the cod, and how they argued and thought through their private business deep in the ocean below.

Long Jack preferred ghost stories. He held the men silent with ghastly tales of spirits on Monomoy Beach that mock and terrify lonely clam diggers. He told of sand-walkers and dune-haunters who were never properly buried, and of Fire Island, a skinny strip of land off the east coast of New York, where dead pirates guarded hidden treasures.

Harvey had always thought that the east coast of America was mostly populated by wealthy people who vacationed there in the summer, relaxing in country houses with hardwood floors. He laughed at the ghost stories, but ended by sitting still and trembling.

Tom Platt went on about his trip around Cape Horn on the old *Ohio*. He told them how red-hot "shots" were loaded into cannons, and would sizzle and flame when they hit wood. And he told how the sailors would throw water on the fires, and yell at the fort to try again. He told of storms and cold that kept two hundred men, night and day, chopping at the ice that covered every rope and plank of wood. He told of nights when the men would gather around the stove and drink cocoa by the bucket. Tom Platt had no use for steam engine ships. His navy service ended when the steamers were still new. He admitted that it was a reasonable invention for peace time, but looked hopefully for the day when sails would return again on tremendous, ten thousand ton ships.

Manuel's talk was slow and gentle—all about pretty girls in Portugal who washed clothes in rivers, by moonlight, under waving banana trees. He told legends of saints, tales of strange dances, and fights in the cold Newfoundland fishing ports. Salters's talk was mainly about farming. His mission in life was to prove the value of natural manure over every form of phosphate fertilizer whatsoever. He grew passionate and angry about phosphates. He dragged greasy books about farming down from his bunk and read from them, wagging his finger at Harvey, who didn't understand a word. Little Penn was so genuinely hurt when Harvey made fun of Salters's lectures that the boy gave it up, and suffered in polite silence. That was very good for Harvey.

The cook did not join in these conversations. As a rule, he spoke only when it was absolutely necessary, but at times a mysterious gift of speech came over him, and he would speak for an hour at a time. He was especially talkative with the boys, and he stood by his prediction that one day Harvey would be Dan's master. He told them about carrying mail in the winter up near Cape Breton, Canada. He described the ram steamer that breaks the ice between the mainland and Prince Edward Island. Then he told them stories that his mother had told him, of life far to the south, where the water never froze. He said that when he died, his soul would go to lie down on a warm white-sand beach with palm trees waving above. To the boys, it seemed like a very odd idea for a man who had never seen a palm tree in his life. Also, at each meal, he would ask Harvey, and Harvey alone, whether the cooking was good. This always made the "second half" laugh. Yet they had a great respect for the cook's judgment, and in their hearts considered Harvey something of a lucky charm themselves.

Harvey was learning new things all the time,

and growing strong and healthy with every gulp of good air. Meanwhile, the *We're Here* went her way and did her business on the Bank. The silvery gray stacks of fish mounted higher and higher, and the men continued their long days of work.

Naturally, a man of Disko's reputation was closely watched by his neighbors, but he had a talent for giving them the slip through the foggy banks. Disko objected to mixed gatherings of a fleet of all nations. Most of them were Gloucester boats, with a few from Provincetown, Rhode Island and some of the Maine ports. But the crewmen on these ships came from goodness knows where. These men were an unpredictable bunch, and when greed is added, there's a fine chance for any kind of accident in the crowded fleet.

"Let the two Jerald brothers lead the fleet," said Disko. "We're bound to lay among the other men fer a while on the Eastern Shoals. If we're lucky, we won't hev to stay long though. Where we are now, Harve, it ain't considered good fishing ground."

"Ain't it?" said Harvey, who was drinking a cup of water after an unusually long dressing-down. "Shouldn't mind striking some poor ground for a change, then."

"Say, Dad," said Dan. "Looks like we won't hev to stay more'n two weeks on the Shoals. You'll meet all the comp'ny you want then, Harve. That's when the real work begins. No regular meals fer no one then, an' sleep when ye can't keep awake. Good thing you wasn't picked up a month later than you was. You wouldn't be in no kind o' shape fer the Old Virgin Rock."

Harvey understood from Disko's fishing chart that this would be the turning point of their trip. The Old Virgin was a tremendous rock that rose nearly to the surface of the water. She was surrounded by a cluster of strangely named "shoals" or shallow waters filled with rock formations. Whales, cod and other fish would gather there to feed on seaweed. With good luck, this is where they would fill the remainder of the storage hold with fish. But seeing the size of the Virgin (it was one tiny dot), he wondered how even Disko could find her. He learned later that Disko was entirely capable in this or any other task, and could even help others. A big four-by-five blackboard hung in the cabin. Harvey never understood the need for it till, after some extremely foggy days, they heard the unpleasant holler of a foot-powered foghorn. It was a machine that bellowed like a sick elephant.

"Square-rigger askin' fer his latitude," said Long Jack. The *We're Here* rang her bell three times, and the larger boat emerged from the fog with shrieks and shouting. It was a large sailing ship with three masts and several rectangular sails.

"Frenchman, from St. Malo," said Uncle

Salters, scornfully. "I'm almost outer tobacco anyway."

"Same here," said Tom Platt. "Hey! Backez vous—backez vous! Git away, you butt-ended Frenchmen! Where you from—St. Malo?"

"Ah! Oui! Oui! St. Malo!," cried the other crowd, waving wool caps and laughing. Then all together, "Board! Board!"

"Bring up the chalk board, Danny. Beats me how them Frenchmen git anywhere without us Americans to help 'em. Forty-six, forty-nine, Dan."

Dan chalked the figures on the board and hung it from the main mast to a chorus of "Merci! Merci!"

"Seems kinder unfriendly to let 'em sail off into nowheres like this," Salters suggested.

"Hev ye learned French since our last trip?" said Disko. "I don't need your bad French gittin' barrels thrown at us like last year."

"We're all dreadful short on tobacco. Young feller, don't you speak French?"

"Oh, yes," said Harvey proudly, and he hollered: "Hi! Say! Arretez vous! Attendez! Nous sommes venant pour tabac."

"Ah, tabac, tabac!" they cried, and laughed again.

"That got 'em. Let's heave a dory over," said Tom Platt. "I don't hold no certificates in French, but I bet I know another language.

Come on, Harve. You interpret."

There was tremendous noise and confusion when he and Harvey were hauled up the side of the ship. The cabin was covered with awful colored pictures of the Virgin Rock—the Virgin of Newfoundland, they called her. Harvey discovered his school-taught French was of no use on the Grand Banks, so he was limited to nods and grins. But Tom Platt waved his arms and made hand gestures, and got along just fine. The captain gave him a drink of gin, and the crew, with their hairy throats, red caps and long knives, greeted him like a brother. Then the trade began. They had plenty of tobacco. They wanted chocolate and crackers. Harvey rowed back to arrange with the cook and Disko. Upon his return, the tins of chocolate and crackers were counted out. The men looked like pirates dividing their loot, and Tom Platt emerged with a bounty of chewing and smoking tobacco. Then those jolly French mariners swung off into the mist, loudly singing together.

"How come my French didn't work, but your sign-talk did?" Harvey demanded when the loot had been distributed among the men.

"Sign-talk?" Platt huffed. "Well, yes, it was sign-talk. But that language is a whole lot older'n your French, Harve. Them French boats are chock full o' Freemasons."

Harvey was stunned. He had heard rumors

of the Freemasons. It was an ancient—and very secretive—society that only invited the very smartest of men to join them. Presidents, generals, wealthy businessmen, even kings were known to be Freemasons. He didn't know much more about them, except for whispers of mysterious rituals and secret codes shared by the members.

"Are you a Freemason, then?" Harvey stammered.

"Looks that way, don't it?" said the Navy man, stuffing his pipe, and Harvey had another mystery of the deep sea to think about.

CHAPTER 6

Harvey was amazed at the extremely casual way in which some ships loafed about the broad Atlantic. Fishing boats, as Dan said, were naturally dependent on the courtesy and wisdom of their neighbors when it came to determining their location. But one expected better things of steamers. That was after another interesting encounter, when they had been chased through the fog for three miles by a big lumbering old cattle boat that smelled like a thousand cows. A very excited officer yelled at them through a speaking trumpet as the steamer bounced helplessly on the water. Disko ran the *We're Here* right alongside her and gave the skipper a piece of his mind.

"Where might ye be, eh? Ye don't deserve to be anywheres. You barnyard boats go hoggin' the road on the high seas with no blame consideration fer your neighbors. Ye keep your eyes in your coffee cups instead o' in your silly heads."

At this the skipper said something about Disko's eerily light-blue eyes. "We haven't seen the stars for three days. Do you suppose we can steer the ship blind?" he shouted.

"Well I can," Disko retorted. "Where's your lead, eh? Can't ye measure water depth? Or are them cattle keeping ye too busy?"

"What d' ye feed 'em?" said Uncle Salters with intense seriousness. The smell of the cows woke the farmer in him. "They say they die off dreadful on a voyage. Dunno as it's any o' my business, but I've an idea that if ye feed 'em a good mixture of . . ."

"Thunder!" said a cattleman in a red jersey as he looked over the side. "What asylum did they let 'ol Whiskers out of?"

"Young feller," Salters began, "let me tell you 'fore we go any further that I'm—"

The officer took off his cap with immense politeness. "Excuse me," he said, "but I've asked for my latitude. If the agricultural person with the hair will kindly shut his mouth, perhaps the crazy-eyed captain will condescend to enlighten us."

"Now you've made a fool o' me, Salters," said Disko, angrily. He could not stand up to that particular sort of talk, and snapped out the latitude and longitude without more lectures.

"Well, that's a boatload of lunatics," said the skipper, as he rang up the engine room and tossed a bundle of newspapers into the schooner.

It was customary to offer a few recent newspapers to a ship that had offered help.

"Of all the blamed fools, next to you, Salters, him an' his crowd are about the likeliest I've ever seen," said Disko as the *We're Here* slid away. "I was jest givin' him my judgment on loafin' round these waters like a lost child, an' you cut in with your fool farmin'. Can't ye ever keep things sep'rate?"

Harvey, Dan, and the others stood back, winking to each other and full of joy. But Disko and Salters quarreled seriously till evening. Salters argued that a cattle boat was practically a barn on blue water, while Disko insisted that, even if this were the case, decency and fisher-pride demanded that he should have kept "things sep'rate." Long Jack tolerated this in silence for a time, but an angry captain makes an unhappy crew. So, after supper was finished, he spoke across the table:

"What's the good o' botherin' with what they'll say about us?" he asked.

"They'll tell that tale against us fer years—that's all," said Disko. "Offerin' yer wisdom on cattle feed! It's plumb mortifyin' to all my feelings."

"Don't see it that way," said Long Jack, the peacemaker. "Look here, Disko! Is there another ship afloat today, in this weather, that could ha' slid alongside a steamer and given those men their latitude? And then, over an' above that, I say, could ha' discuss'd with them, quite intelligent, the management of cattle at sea? Forgit it! Those men won't be so lucky agin, the way I see it."

Dan kicked Harvey under the table, and Harvey choked in his cup.

"Well," said Salters, who felt that his honor had been somewhat restored, "I said I didn't know if it was any o' my business, before I spoke."

"An' right there," said Tom Platt, experienced in discipline and manners, "right there, I take it, Disko, you should ha' asked him to stop talkin' ef the conversation wuz likely, in your jedgment, to be anyways—what it shouldn't."

"Well, I suppose that's right," said Disko, who saw his way to an honorable retreat from the argument.

"Why, o' course it's right," said Salters, "you bein' skipper here. I'd hev stopped at once, if fer no other reason, fer the sake o' being an example to these two blame boys of ours."

"Didn't I tell you, Harve, it would come around to us 'fore long? Always those blame boys. But I wouldn't have missed the show fer anything," Dan whispered.

"Still, things should ha' been kept sep'rate," said Disko, and the light of new argument lit in Salters' eye as he crumbled tobacco into his pipe.

"There's a power of virtue in keepin' things

sep'rate," said Long Jack, intent on quieting the storm. "That's what a business man named Steyning found out when he hired Nick Counahan as skipper on the ship called *Marilla*. Counahan the Navigator, we called him."

"Nick Counahan! Well, he never went aboard fer a night without a pond o' rum with him," said Tom Platt, following Long Jack's lead. "Counahan the Navigator! Dead fer fifteen years, ain't he?"

"Seventeen, I guess. He could never keep things sep'rate. Steyning took him on fer the same reason a thief takes a hot stove—'cause there was nothin' else around that season. Counahan put together a mighty rough crowd fer the crew. Then there wuz the rum. Ye could ha' paid fer the *Marilla* herself, insurance an' all, with the amount o' rum they had aboard her. They left Boston Harbor for the great Grand Banks with a roarin' storm behind 'em. But the heavens looked after 'em, since those men didn't stand one watch, and they didn't lay one single hand on a rope, till they'd seen the bottom of every fifteen gallon cask of rum aboard. It took 'em about one week, so far as Counahan remembered. (If I cud only tell the tale as he told it!) All that whole time the wind blew like old glory, an' the *Marilla*, she jus' found her stride an' stuck to it. Then Counahan took the hog yoke and trembled over it for a while. Between that an' the chart and the singin' in his head, he figured they was just south o' Sable Island. They were getting along gloriously, so they cracked open another keg o' rum and quit worrying about anythin' for another spell."

"The *Marilla* kept on her course, but the men saw no sea gulls or schooners, and presently they observed they'd been out fer fourteen days. So, they dropped their lead an' measured sixty fathom. 'That's me,' sez Counahan. 'That's me every time! I've run her straight to the Banks fer you. When we get thirty fathom we'll drop our lines. Counahan's the one,' he sez. 'Counahan the Navigator!'

"Nex' time they drop the lead, they got ninety. Sez Counahan: 'Either the lead line's took to stretchin' or else the Bank's sunk.'

The *Marilla* set out agin, and along came a steamer, an' Counahan spoke to her.

"'Hev ye seen any fishin' boats?' he sez, quite casual."

"'There's lots uv them off the Irish coast,' sez the steamer."

"'Aah! Go shake yerself,' sez Counahan. 'What do I care about the Irish coast?'"

"'Then what are ye doin' here?' sez the steamer."

"'Sufferin' Christianity!' sez Counahan. Where am I?'"

"'Thirty-five mile west-southwest o' Cape

Clear, on the southern tip o' Ireland,' sez the steamer, 'if that's any consolation to you.'"

"Counahan nearly jumped out o' his boots."

"'Consolation!' sez he, bold as ever. 'Thirty-five mile from Cape Clear, an' fourteen days from Boston? Sufferin' Christianity, 'tis a record! We've set a record, men!' Can ye imagine the nerve o' him? Proud as ever that he'd sailed his men clear 'cross the ocean, and nowhere close to where they was aimin' for. Ye see, Counahan could never keep things sep'rate.

"The crew was mostly men from Ireland, an' they ran the old *Marilla* right into an Irish port town. They had a grand ol' time visitin' around with friends fer a week. Then they set sail, an' it took 'em thirty-two days to git through the Banks again. 'Twas gettin' on towards fall by that time, and food was low, so Counahan ran her back to Boston without one fish on board."

"And what did his boss say?" Harvey demanded.

"What could he say? The fish was in the Banks, an' Counahan was in Boston, talkin' 'bout his record trip east! An' all on account of not keepin' the crew and the rum sep'rate in the first place; an' confusin' Cape Clear with the Grand Banks, in the second. Counahan the Navigator, rest his soul!

"Once I was in the ship called *Lucy Holmes*," said Manuel, in his gentle voice. "They not want any of her fish in Gloucester. They give us no price. So we go across the water, and think to sell to some man on the islands off Portugal. Then de storm comes, and we cannot see well. Soon we all go down below and drive very fast—no one know where. By and by we see a land. Then come two, three black men in a boat. Eh, wha-at? We ask where we are, and guess what they say?"

"Grand Canary Island," said Disko, after a moment. Manuel shook his head, smiling.

"No. Worse than that. We was just off the coast of Liberia! Africa! So we sell our fish there!"

"My father, he run his boat over to Greenland's icy mountains," said Disko. "An' what's more, he took my mother along with him, to show her how the money was earned, I presume. They got stuck in the ice, an' I was born on Disko Island. Don't remember nothin' about it, o' course. We come back when the ice eased in the spring, but they named me fer the place. Kind of a mean trick to put upon a baby, but we're all bound to make mistakes in our lives."

"Sure! Sure!" said Salters, wagging his head. "All bound to make mistakes. I tell you two boys here thet after you've made a mistake—and ye don't make fewer'n a hundred a day—the best thing's to own up to it like men."

Long Jack winked one tremendous wink that embraced all the men except Disko and Salters, and the incident was closed.

Then they made their way northward. The dories were out almost every day, running along the east edge of the Grand Banks, and fishing steadily.

It was here that Harvey first met the squid. It is one of the best cod baits, but a very moody creature. One black night, they were awoken from their bunks by yells of "Squid, ho!" from Salters. For an hour and a half, every soul aboard hung over his "squid jig"—a piece of fishing line painted red and armed at the end with a circle of pins bent backward like half-opened umbrella. For some unknown reason, the squid loves this thing and wraps himself round it. The squid is then hauled up into the boat. But as he leaves the ocean, he squirts water, and then ink, into his captor's face.

It was curious to see the men weaving their heads from side to side to dodge the shot. They were all covered with ink when the fight ended; but a pile of fresh squid lay on the deck. The large cod thinks very well of a little shiny piece of squid tentacle at the tip of a baited hook. The next day they caught many fish, and met the ship named *Carrie Pitman*, to whom they shouted their luck. The Carrie crew wanted to trade seven cod for one fair-sized squid, but Disko would not agree to the price. So, the *Carrie* moved on, and anchored half a mile away in the hope of catching some squid for herself.

Disko said nothing till after supper, when he sent Dan and Manuel out to tie a buoy to the anchor cable. This was a strange request, usually reserved for when the boat was dropping anchor on a rocky bottom. If the anchor slips on a rock and a boat begins to drift, sometimes the cable must be cut in order to steer the ship to safety. Without a buoy attached, the anchor and cable would disappear forever at the bottom of the ocean. In this case, however, Disko was thinking of the *Carrie Pitman*, which had an ugly reputation for breaking free of her own anchor and drifting right into her neighbors. Dan naturally repeated Disko's worries to the dory from the *Carrie*, who wanted to know why they were setting a buoy.

"Dad sez he wouldn't trust a ferryboat within five mile o' you," Dan howled cheerfully.

"She ain't driftin' any this trip," said the man angrily.

"Then how d'you catch fish?" said Dan. "Driftin' is her best chance, with yer crew in charge. Ye don't know where to look for fish, so ye might as well drift to 'em." That shot went home.

"Hey, you Portugese organ grinder, take your monkey back to Gloucester. Go back to school, Dan Troop," was the answer.

"O-ver-alls! O-ver-alls!" yelled Dan, who knew that one of the Carrie's crew had worked in an overall factory the winter before.

"Shrimp! Gloucester shrimp!"

Dan answered in kind. "Shrimp yourself, ye Chatham wreckers! Git out o' here with your brick ship!" And the forces separated.

"I know how it will be," said Disko. "She'll stay put till midnight, an' jest when we're gettin' our sleep she'll strike adrift. Good thing we ain't crowded with ships over here."

The wind picked up at sundown and blew steadily. Although the wind was not strong enough to disturb a dory, the *Carrie Pitman* was a law unto herself. At the end of the boys' watch they heard a crack-crack-crack in the distance.

"Glory, glory, hallelujah!" sung Dan. "Here she comes, Dad! Butt-end first, walkin' in her sleep."

Had she been any other boat, Disko would have taken his chances. But now he cut the anchor cable as the *Carrie Pitman* stumbled directly towards them. The *We're Here* gave her no more room than was absolutely necessary, as the *Carrie* passed within arm's length of the men. It was a silent and angry boat, helpless at the mercy of the sea.

"Good evenin'," said Disko. "An' where might ye be headed?"

"Go to Ohio an' hire a mule," said Uncle Salters. "We don't want no farmers here."

"Should I lend you my dory anchor?" cried Long Jack.

"Say!" cried Dan in his high-pitched voice. "Sa-ay! Is there a strike in the overall factory, or hev they hired girls?"

The following day, the men wasted half the morning recovering the anchor cable, which hung on the end of the floating buoy. But the boys agreed the trouble was cheap at the price of triumph and glory. They thought for a long while about all the beautiful things they might have said to the humiliated *Carrie*.

CHAPTER 7

The next day, they fell in with more ships, all circling slowly from the east towards the west. But just when they expected to make the shoals by the Virgin Rock, the fog rolled in. The men dropped anchor, surrounded by the jingle of invisible bells. There was not much fishing, but occasionally, dory met dory in the fog and exchanged news.

Dan and Harvey had been sleeping most of the day. That night, a little before dawn, the boys snuck out to "pirate" a few fried pies. They could have simply asked for the pies, but they tasted better when stolen. Plus, it made the cook angry. The boys took their plunder to the upper deck where they found Disko at the bell, which he handed over to Harvey.

"Keep her goin'," he said. "I think I hear somethin'. If it's what I suspect, it's best to stay where we are."

The bell made a sad little jingle, which the thick air seemed to swallow up. In the distance,

Harvey heard the muffled shriek of a passenger ship's siren, and he knew enough of the Grand Banks to know what that meant. He remembered, with horrible clarity, how a boy in a cherry-colored blazer (he hated fancy blazers now, with all a fisherman's disgust), how an ignorant, rowdy boy had once said it would be "great" if a steamer ran over a fishing boat. That boy had a private room with a hot and cold bath. That boy spent ten minutes each morning examining his gold-colored, first-class ticket. And that same boy was now awake at four o'clock in the morning, hammering away for dear life on a bell smaller than the waiter's breakfast bell.

Meanwhile, somewhere close by, a huge steel ship was storming along at twenty miles an hour! The bitterest thought of all was that there were folks asleep in dry, beautiful cabins who would never know that they had massacred a boat before breakfast. So Harvey rang the bell.

"Sure, they can slow down with one turn o' their blame propeller," said Dan, holding Manuel's conch shell. "But that ain't consolin' when we're all at the bottom o' the sea. Ring, Harve! She's movin' fast!"

"Aooo-whoo!" went the siren. "Tingle-tink," went the bell. "Graaa-ouch!" went the conch in the milky fog. Then Harvey felt that he was near a moving body. He looked up to see the tremendous, cliff-like side of a passenger ship. It

seemed to hang directly over the schooner.
Harvey could make out the peach-colored paint,
and the round brass rims of the porthole windows as it passed by. It tilted forward and down-
ward with a terrifying "hisss," until a jet of steam
puffed in Harvey's face and a spout of hot engine
water roared onto the decks of the *We're Here*.
The little schooner staggered and shook in a rush
of propeller-torn water, as the steamer vanished
in the fog. Harvey got ready to faint or be sick,
or both, when he heard a loud crack, like the
snapping of a tree. Then, a small faraway voice
yelled: "Heave to! You've sunk us!"

"Is it us?" he gasped.

"No! Boat out yonder. Ring, Harve! We're
goin' to look," said Dan, lowering a dory.

In thirty seconds, all except Harvey, Penn
and the cook were over the side and on their way.
A schooner's foremast, snapped clean in half,
drifted past. Then an empty green dory came by,
knocking on the side of the *We're Here*'s as
though she wished to be taken in. Then followed
something, face down, in a blue jersey. It was the
body of a man. Penn changed color and gasped.
Harvey pounded despairingly at the bell, for he
feared they might be sunk at any minute, and he
jumped at Dan's holler as the crew came back.

"The *Jennie Cushman*," said Dan, hysterical-
ly, "cut clean in half. Ground up an' trampled on
at that! Not a quarter of a mile away. Dad's got

the old man. There ain't anyone else, and—there was his son, too. Oh, Harve, Harve, I can't stand it! I've seen—" He dropped his head on his arms and sobbed while the others dragged a gray-headed man aboard.

"What did you pick me up for?" the stranger groaned. "Disko, what did you pick me up for?"

Disko dropped a heavy hand on his shoulder, for the man's eyes were wild and his lips trembled as he stared at the silent crew. Then Pennsylvania Pratt stood up, and spoke. His face was changed from the face of a fool to that of an old, wise man. He said in a strong voice: "The Lord gave, and the Lord hath taken away; blessed be the name of the Lord! I was—I am a minister of the Gospel. Leave him to me."

"Oh, is that what ye be?" said the man. "Then pray my son back to me! Pray back a nine thousand dollar boat an' a hundred thousand pounds of fish. If you'd left me alone my widow could ha' gone on and never known. Never known! Now I'll hev to tell her."

"There ain't nothin' to say," said Disko. "Better lie down a piece, Jason Olley."

When a man has lost his only son, his summer's work, and his means of livelihood, all in thirty seconds, it is hard to give comfort.

"All Gloucester men, wasn't they?" said Tom Platt, fiddling helplessly with a dory rope.

Jason squeezed the water from his beard.

"I'll be rowin' rich vacationers 'round East Gloucester this fall." He leaned heavily on the railing of the *We're Here*.

"Come with me. Come below!" said Penn, as though he had a right to give orders. Their eyes met for a quarter of a minute, and Jason glared at Penn suspiciously.

"I dunno who you be, but I'll come," Jason

said at last. "Mebbe I'll get back some o' the . . . some o' the nine thousand dollars." Penn led him into the cabin and slid the door closed.

"That ain't Penn," cried Uncle Salters. "It's Jacob Boiler, an' he's remembered Johnstown! I never seen such eyes in any livin' man's head. What's to do now? What'll I do now?"

They could hear Penn's voice and Jason's together. Then Penn's went on alone, and Salters slipped off his hat, for Penn was praying. Then the little man came up the steps. There were huge drops of sweat on his face, and he looked at the crew. Dan was still sobbing by the wheel.

"He don't know us," Salters groaned. "We'll hev to start all over again, checkers and everything. And what'll he say to me?"

Penn spoke. They could tell that he did not know who they were. "I have prayed," he said. "Our people believe in prayer. I have prayed for the life of this man's son. Mine were drowned before my eyes—she and my eldest and—the others. I never prayed for their lives. But I have prayed for this man's son, and God will surely return him."

Salters looked desperately at Penn to see if he remembered.

"How long have I been mad?" Penn asked suddenly. His mouth was twitching.

"Aww, Penn! You weren't never mad," Salters began "Only a little distracted like."

"I saw the houses hit the bridge before the fires broke out. I do not remember any more. How long ago is that?"

"I can't stand it! I can't stand it!" cried Dan, and Harvey whimpered in sympathy.

"About five year," said Disko, in a shaking voice.

"Then I have been a burden on someone every day since then. Someone has taken care of me. Who was the man?"

Disko pointed to Salters.

"Ye ain't a burden. Ye ain't!" cried the sea farmer, twisting his hands together. "Ye've more than earned yer keep. An' there's money owed to you, Penn, besides half o' my quarter share in the boat."

"You are good men. I can see that in your faces. But—"

"Mother o' Mercy," whispered Long Jack, "an' he's been with us all these trips! He's clean bewitched."

A schooner's bell rang alongside, and a voice hollered through the fog: "O Disko! Heard about the *Jennie Cushman*?"

"They have found his son," cried Penn. "Stand you still and see the salvation of the Lord!"

"Got Jason aboard here," Disko answered, but his voice wavered. "There . . . wasn't any one else?"

"We've found a survivor. 'Run across him snarled up in a mess o' lumber. His head's cut some."

"Who is he?"

Every heartbeat on the *We're Here* stood still.

"Guess it's young Olley," the voice said casually.

Penn raised his hands and said something in Latin. Harvey could have sworn that a bright light was shining upon his face. But the voice went on: "Sa-ay! You fellers insulted us somethin' fierce the other night."

"We don't feel like insultin' any now," said Disko.

"I know it. But to tell the honest truth, we was kind of . . . kind of driftin' when we run against young Olley."

It was the unstoppable *Carrie Pitman*, and a roar of laughter went up from the deck of the *We're Here*.

"Why don't ye send the old man aboard? Guess you don't need him anyway, an' all this blame windlass work makes us short-handed. We'll take care of him. He's married to my wife's aunt."

"I'll give you anything in the boat," said Troop.

"Don't want nothin', 'cept maybe an anchor that'll hold. Say! Young Olley's gittin' kind of excited. Send the old man along."

Penn waked Jason from his stupor of despair, and Tom Platt rowed him over. He went away without a word of thanks, not knowing what was to come, and the fog closed over him.

"And now," said Penn, drawing a deep breath as though he was about to preach. "And now . . ." His body sank and the light faded from his bright eyes. His voice returned to its usual, timid tone. "And now," said Pennsylvania Pratt, "do you think it's too early for a little game of checkers, Mr. Salters?"

"The very thing—the very thing I was goin' to say myself," cried Salters. "It beats everything, Penn, how ye can't figure what's in a man's mind."

The little fellow blushed and quietly followed Salters below deck.

"Up anchor! Hurry! Let's quit these crazy waters," shouted Disko. The men were never so happy to obey him.

"Now what in creation was all that about?" said Long Jack, as they were sailing through the fog once again, damp, dripping, and bewildered.

"The way I figure," said Disko, at the wheel, "it was the *Jennie Cushman* business comin' on an empty stomach—"

"He—he saw one of them go by," sobbed Harvey.

"An' that, o' course, kind of shook him to rememberin' Johnstown an' Jacob Boiler an' such recollections. Well, comfortin' Jason propped him up for a while. Then, bein' weak, them props slipped and slipped, and now he's slid right back to where he was. That's what I figure.

They decided that Disko was entirely correct.

"Would have broken Salters' heart," said Long Jack, "if Penn had stayed Jacob Boiler. Did ye see his face when Penn asked who'd been takin' care of him all these years? How is he, Salters?"

"Asleep—dead asleep. Turned in like a child," Salters replied, tiptoeing across the deck. "There won't be no grub till he wakes, o' course. Don't want no one wakin' him up. Did ye ever see such a gift in prayer? He pulled young Olley straight from the ocean."

They waited three hours, until Penn reappeared with a smooth face and a blank mind. He said he thought he had been dreaming. Then he wanted to know why they were so silent, and they could not tell him.

Disko worked the men mercilessly for the next three or four days. When they could not go out in the dories, he sent them down below to make room for more fish. Disko showed them how to arrange cargo in a way that keeps the schooner balanced. The crew was kept busy with these tasks until they recovered their spirits. Harvey was tickled with a rope's end by Long Jack for being, as the Galway man said, "sad as a

sick cat over something that couldn't be helped."
Harvey did a great deal of thinking in those
weary days, and shared his thoughts with Dan,
who agreed with him. The boys even decided
that from now on, they would ask for fried pies
instead of stealing them.

But a week later, the two nearly sunk the
Hattie S. in a wild attempt to stab a shark with an
old knife tied to a stick. The large shark rubbed
alongside the dory begging for small fish, and
between the three of them, it was a miracle they
all got out alive.

At last there came a morning when Disko
shouted below deck: "Hurry, boys! We're in
town!"

CHAPTER 8

To the end of his days, Harvey would never forget that sight. The red sunrise colored the sails of three full fleets of anchored schooners—one to the north, one to the west, and one to the south. There must have been nearly a hundred ships of every possible make and build, all bowing and nodding to each other. From every boat, dories were dropping away like bees from a crowded hive. The racket of voices, the rattling of ropes, and the splash of the oars carried for miles across the water. The sails turned every color imaginable as the sun rose; and more boats swung up through the mists from the south.

The dories gathered in clusters, separated, reformed, and broke up again, all heading in the same direction. The men hollered and whistled and sang, and the water was speckled with garbage thrown overboard.

"It's a town," said Harvey. "Disko was right. It IS a town!"

"I've seen smaller," said Disko. "There's

about a thousand men here; an' yonder's the Virgin Rock." He pointed to an open space of greenish sea, where there were no dories.

The *We're Here* skirted around the northern edge of the crowd as Disko waved to friend after friend. Questions and answers flew back and forth. Men had met one another before, dory fishing in the fog, and there is no place for gossip like the Banks fishing fleet. They all seemed to know about Harvey's rescue, and asked if he was worth his salt yet. Manuel's countrymen jabbered at him in their own language; and even the silent cook was seen shouting to a friend as black as himself. After they had buoyed the anchor cable (the sea around the Virgin is full of rocks), their dories went forth to join the mob of boats anchored about a mile away. The schooners rocked and dipped at a safe distance, like mother ducks watching their babes, while the dories behaved like mischievous ducklings.

As they drove into the confusion, boat banging boat, Harvey's ears burned from the comments about his rowing. Every language from Portuguese and Italian, to French and Gaelic, with songs and shouts, rattled around him. For the first time in his life, Harvey felt shy. He could only stare at the sea of wild faces, waving arms and bare chests tht rose and sank before him.

"Watch out!" said Dan, holding out a fishing net "When I tell you to dip, you dip. The caplin will school any time now. Where'll we lay anchor, Tom Platt?"

Tom Platt led his little fleet to the front of the crowd. Pushing, shoving, and hauling all the way, he greeted old friends and warned old enemies. Three or four men began to haul in their anchors with the intent to cut off the *We're Here*'s boat. But a yell of laughter went up as a dory shot forward suddenly, and very quickly. Its helpless occupant pulled wildly at the anchor line.

"Give her slack!" roared twenty voices. "Let him shake it off!"

"What's the matter?" said Harvey, as the boat flashed by. "He's anchored, isn't he?"

"Sure enough, but his anchor's kind of shifty," said Dan, laughing. "A whale's caught on it. Dip, Harve! Here they come!"

The sea around them clouded and darkened, and then fizzed up with thousands of tiny silver fish called "caplin." They are a favorite food source for cod, and within seconds the larger fish began to leap from the water. Beyond the cod, three or four large, gray-back whales broke the water into big boiling circles.

Then everybody shouted and tried to haul up anchor to get among the school of fish. The men tangled their neighbors' lines, dipped their nets furiously, and shrieked warnings and advice to their companions. All the while, the deep sea fizzed like freshly opened soda. Together, cod,

men and whales flung themselves upon their
unlucky bait. Harvey was nearly knocked overboard by the handle of Dan's net. But in all the
wild chaos, he noticed the wicked little eye of a
whale that swam alongside and (according to
Harvey), winked at him. Three boats found their
anchor lines snagged by these sea hunters, and
were pulled for half a mile before the whales
finally shook the line free.

Then the caplin moved off, and five minutes
later there was no sound except the splash of fishing lines, the flapping of cod, and the whack of
the "muckle" hammers. It was wonderful fishing.
Harvey could see the glimmering cod below,
swimming slowly in groups. Grand Banks law
strictly forbids more than one hook on one line
when the dories are fishing the Virgin Rock or

Eastern Shoals. However, the boats were so close that even single hooks tangled, and Harvey found himself in the middle of a hot argument between a gentle, hairy Newfoundlander on one side, and a howling Portuguese on the other.

Worse than tangled fishing lines was the confusion of the anchor lines below water. Each man had anchored where it seemed good to him, drifting and rowing round his fixed point. As the fish stopped biting, each man wanted to haul up and find better ground. But every third man found himself intimately connected with some four or five neighbors. To cut another man's anchor line is an unspeakable crime on the Banks. Yet it was done, and done many times that day. Tom Platt caught a Maine man in the act and knocked him over with an oar. Manuel punished a fellow countryman in the same way. But Harvey's anchor line was cut, and so was Penn's, and they were turned into relief boats to carry fish to the *We're Here* as the dories filled. The caplin schooled once more at twilight, when the mad chaos was repeated. At dusk they rowed back to dress down by the light of kerosene lamps. It was a huge pile, and they went to sleep while standing at the tables.

The next day several boats fished right above the top of the Virgin Rock, which rose to within twenty feet of the water's surface. Harvey went with them, and looked down on the seaweed that covered the lonely rock. The cod were there in legions, feeding on the leathery "kelp" that covered the Virgin. At noon, the dories took a break and began to search for amusement. It was Dan who spotted the schooner named *Hope of Prague*. He was just coming up, and as her dories joined the company they were greeted with the question: "Who's the meanest man in the fleet?"

Three hundred voices answered cheerily: "Nick Bra-ady."

"Who stole the lamp wicks?" That was Dan's contribution.

"Nick Bra-ady," sang the boats.

"Who boiled the salt fer soup?" This was an unknown fisherman a quarter of a mile away.

Again the joyful chorus. Now, Brady was not especially mean, but he had that reputation, and the fleet made the most of it. Then they discovered a man from an English boat who had once been caught using a line with five or six hooks—a "scrowger," they call it—in the Shoals. Naturally, he had been nicknamed "Scrowger Jim" and he found his title waiting for him as he rowed passed. "Jim! O Jim! Jim! O Jim! Ssscrowger Jim!" sang the men. Every schooner and nearly every man got it in turn. Was there a careless or dirty cook anywhere? The dories sang about him and his food. Had a man stolen tobacco from a shipmate? He was named by the men, and the name was tossed from boat to boat. Disko's flawless judgments, Dan's sweetheart Hattie (oh, was Dan an angry boy!), Penn's bad luck with dory anchors, Salter's views on fertilizer, and Harvey's clumsy way of rowing—all were laid before the public. As the fog fell around them once again, the voices sounded like a bench of invisible judges handing down sentences.

The dories fished and argued until a wave swept across the sea. Then the boats moved away from each other to make sure they didn't collide. Someone yelled that if the waves continued, they would break right over the top of the Virgin Rock. A reckless Galway man disagreed, hauled up anchor, and rowed over the very rock itself. Many voices yelled for them to move away, while others dared them to hold on. As the smooth-backed waves passed to the south, they lifted the dory higher and higher into the mist. Then the dory dropped into the rough water, where she spun around her anchor within a foot or two of the hidden rock. He was playing with death, and the boats looked on in uneasy silence. Finally, Long Jack rowed up behind his countryman and quietly cut his anchor line.

"Can't ye hear it knockin' on yer boat?" he cried. "Row fer yer miserable life! Row!"

The man swore and tried to argue as the boat drifted and the next wave rolled in. There was a sucking noise and a gathering roar as the fast-moving water approached and hit the rock. Then the Virgin flung a wall of white foaming water straight up, and over the sea. All the boats greatly applauded Long Jack, and the Galway man held his tongue.

"Ain't it beautiful?" said Dan, bobbing like a young seal at home.

"Harve, you've seen the greatest thing on the Banks. If not for Long Jack, you'd seen some dead men too. She'll roar like that every fifteen minutes or so, dependin' on the tide an' weather."

There came a sound of laughter where the fog was thicker and the schooners were ringing their bells. A big schooner crept cautiously out of the mist, and was received with shouts and cries of, "Come along, darlin'," from the Irish.

"Is she a Frenchman?" said Harvey, noticing the square sails of the ship.

"Ain't you got eyes? She's a Baltimore boat, creepin' ahead with fear an' tremblin'," said Dan. "We'll tease the very sticks out of her. Guess it's the first time her skipper ever met up with the fleet this way."

She was a black, curvy, eight hundred ton craft. Her main sail was rolled up, and her top sail flapped nervously in what little wind was moving. She was a tall and feminine creature, and looked just like a confused woman half-lifting her skirt to cross a muddy street. She knew she was somewhere in the neighborhood of the Virgin and was, therefore, asking for directions. This is a small part of what she heard from the dancing dories:

"The Virgin? What are ye talkin' about? 'This is the French Coast on a Sunday mornin'. Go home an' sober up."

A wave rolled by, and the front of the ship dipped dangerously low into the water.

"Raise yer sails! Raise 'em!"

"No, lower yer sails! Lower 'em!"

"Down jib!"

"Up foresail!"

Here the skipper lost his temper and said things. Instantly fishing was suspended to answer him. They asked him if he was insured, and whether he had stolen his anchor, because, they said, it belonged to the *Carrie Pitman*. They called his boat a mud-cow, and accused him of dumping garbage to frighten the fish. They offered to tow him and charge it to his wife; and one bold youth slipped up to the ship's rear, smacked it with his hand, and yelled, "Giddee-up, horsey!"

They would have warned her at once had she been in real danger. But, seeing that she was well clear of the Virgin Rock, they made the most of the opportunity. The fun was spoiled when the tormented ship set every sail she had and went her way. But, the dories felt that victory was theirs.

The Virgin Rock roared all night, and the

next morning brought an angry, stormy sea. Harvey awoke to find the fleet waiting, their masts bouncing on the horizon. Not a single dory was lowered until ten o'clock, when the two Jeralds of the *Day's Eye* imagined a pause in the storm that did not exist. They headed out, and in a minute half the dories were following their lead, bobbing in the swells. Troop kept the men of the *We're Here* at work dressing down. He saw no sense in "dares." Sure enough, as the storm grew that evening, they had the pleasure of receiving wet strangers who were only too glad to take shelter. The boys stood by the dory ropes with lanterns, the men ready to haul up the stranded strangers. All the while, they kept one eye on the sweeping waves that would make them drop everything and hold on for dear life. Out of the dark would come a yell of "Dory, dory!" They would hook up and haul in a drenched man and a half-sunk boat, till their decks were littered with dories and the bunks were full. Five separate times, Harvey and Dan found themselves clinging to ropes and soaked sails as a huge wave filled the decks. One dory was smashed to pieces, and the sea pitched the man headfirst on to the decks, cutting his forehead open. At dawn, another man, whose face was blue and ghost-like, crawled in with a broken hand, asking news of his brother. Seven extra mouths sat down to breakfast: A Swede; a Chatham skipper; a boy from Hancock,

Maine; and four Provincetown men.

There was a general sorting out among the fleet next day. No one said a word, but all the men ate with better appetites as boat after boat reported full crews. A couple of Portuguese and an old man from Gloucester were drowned, and many were cut or bruised. Two schooners had been blown to the south and would need at least three days to sail back. A man died on a Frenchman—the same schooner that had traded tobacco with the *We're Here*. She slipped away quietly one morning, moved to a patch of deep water, and Harvey watched the funeral through Disko's spy glass. It was only a long bundle slid over the ship's side. They did not seem to have any type of formal service, but during the night, Harvey heard them across the starlit water, singing something that sounded like a slow, mournful hymn.

Tom Platt visited her, because, he said, the dead man was his brother as a Freemason. It came out that a wave had thrown the poor fellow against the boom and broken his back. The news spread like a flash since the Frenchman held an auction of the dead man's belongings. He had no friends in St. Malo, so everything was spread out on the decks, from his red knitted cap to the leather belt with a knife fastened to the back. Dan and Harvey were out in the *Hattie S.*, and naturally rowed over to join the crowd. Dan bought the knife and belt, which had a curious brass handle. When they climbed back into the dory and pushed off into a drizzle of rain, it occurred to them that they might get into trouble for neglecting their fishing.

"Guess it won't hurt us any to be warmed up by a rope's end," said Dan, shivering under his oilskins. They rowed on into the heart of a white fog, which, as usual, dropped on them without warning.

"The tide's too strong to trust your instincts," he said. "Heave over the anchor, Harve, and we'll fish a while till the fog lifts."

The boys could not see a boat's length in any direction. Harvey turned up his collar and bunched himself over his fishing reel like a weary navigator. They fished a while in silence. Then Dan drew the knife and examined it.

"That's a beauty," said Harvey. "How did you get it so cheap?"

"On account o' their blame Catholic superstitions," said Dan, jabbing with the bright blade. "They don't like takin' weapons off a dead man. Did ye see them Frenchmen step back when I bid?"

"But an auction ain't disrespectful to the dead. It's just business."

"We know that, but there's no talkin' with superstition. That's one o' the advantages o' livin' in a progressive country."

"Why didn't that Eastport man bid, then? He bought the Frenchman's boots. Ain't Maine progressive?"

"Maine? They don't even know enough, or they ain't got money enough, to paint their houses in Maine. I've seen 'em! The Eastport man told me that the knife had been "used" up on the French coast. So the French captain told him."

"To cut a man?" Harvey hauled in a fish, rebaited, and threw the line back over.

"Killed him! Course, when I heard that, I jus' had to get it."

"Christmas!" said Harvey, turning around. "I'll give you a dollar for it when I—get my wages. Say, I'll give you two dollars."

"Honest? D'you like it that much?" said Dan, blushing. "Well, to tell the truth, I kinder got it for you, but I didn't let on till I saw how you'd take it. It's yours, Harve, because we're dorymates, and so on."

He held out the knife, belt and all.

"But look here. Dan, I don't see—"

"Take it. 'Tain't no use to me. I want you to hev it."

The temptation was irresistible. "Dan," said Harvey, "I'll keep it as long as I live."

"That's good to hear," said Dan, with a laugh. Then, anxious to change the subject: "'Look's if your line got hold of somethin'."

"Tangled, I guess," said Harve, tugging. Before he pulled up he fastened the knife belt around him. With deep delight, he heard the weapon click against the boat.

"I can't pull it up!" he cried. "Feels like a batch of jellyfish, but they don't swim here, do they?"

Dan reached over and gave a tug at the line. "Sick Halibut, mebbe. That's no jellyfish. Guess we better haul her up to make sure."

They pulled together, and the mysterious weight rose slowly.

"Haul!" shouted Dan, but the shout ended in a double shriek of horror. Out of the sea came the body of the dead Frenchman buried two days before! The hook had caught him under the right armpit, and he swayed head and shoulders above water. His arms were tied to his side, and—he had no face. The boys fell over each other in a heap at the bottom of the dory as the thing bobbed alongside.

"The tide—the tide brought him!" said Harvey with quivering lips, as he fumbled with the belt.

"Oh, Lord! Oh, Harve!" groaned Dan. "Be quick. He's come for his knife. Let him have it. Take it off."

"I don't want it! I don't want it!" cried Harvey. "I can't find the bu-buckle."

"Quick, Harve! He's on your line!"

Harvey sat up to unfasten the belt, facing the head that had no face under its streaming hair. Dan slipped out his knife and cut the fishing line, as Harvey flung the belt far into the water. The body shot down with a plop, and Dan cautiously rose to his knees, whiter than the fog.

"He come for it. He come for it. I've seen a dead body hauled up on a trawl line once, and I didn't much care. But this man, he come to us on purpose."

"I wish—I wish I hadn't taken the knife. Then he'd have come on your line," stammered Harvey.

"Dunno as thet would ha' made any difference. We're both scared out o' ten years' growth. Oh, Harve, did ye see his head?"

"Did I? I'll never forget it. But look at here, Dan, it couldn't have been on purpose. It was only the tide."

"Tide! He come for it, Harve. Why, they sunk him six miles south o' the fleet. They told me he was weighted down with chain cable."

"Wonder what he did with the knife—up on the French coast?"

"Something bad. Guess he has to take it with him to his judgment 'fore the almighty and such."

The boys sat in silence for a few moments.

"I'd give a month's pay if this fog 'u'd lift," said Dan. "Ye see things in the fog that ye don't see in clear weather. I'm sort of relieved he come the way he did, instead o' walkin'. He might ha' walked."

"Don't, Dan! We're right on top of him now. I wish I was safe on the ship, getting holler'd at by Salters."

"They'll be lookin' fer us soon. Gimme the horn." Dan took the tin dinner horn, but paused before he blew.

"Go on," said Harvey. "I don't want to stay here all night"

"A man from down the Massachusetts coast told me once he was in a schooner where they wouldn't dare blow a horn to the dories. He said an old captain of theirs had drowned a boy in a drunken fit. Ever since, that boy would row alongside and shout, 'Dory! Dory!' every time the horn blew."

"Dory! dory!" a muffled voice cried through the fog. They trembled again, and the horn dropped from Dan's hand.

"Hold on!" cried Harvey; "it's the cook."

"Dunno what made me think o' that fool story, either," said Dan. "It's the cook, sure enough."

"Dan! Danny! Oooh, Dan! Harve! Harvey! Oooh, Haarveee!"

We're Here, sung both boys together. They heard oars, but couldn't see anything till the cook, shining and dripping, rowed into them.

"What has happened?" said he. "You will be

beaten at home."

"That's what we want," said Dan. "Anything homey's good enough fer us. We've had kinder depressin' company." As the cook passed them a tow line, Dan told him the tale.

"Yes! He come for his knife," was all the cook said at the end.

The cook rowed them back, and the *We're Here* never looked so deliciously home-like to the boys. There was a warm glow of light from the cabin and a satisfying smell of food. It was heavenly to hear Disko and the others leaning over the rail and promising them a first-class pounding. But the cook was a master of strategy. He did not get the dories aboard till he had told the men about the dead Frenchmen. As he bumped and backed up his dory, he explained how Harvey was the lucky charm to destroy any possible bad luck. So the boys came aboard as heroes, and everyone asked them questions instead of pounding them for making trouble. Little Penn delivered quite a speech on the foolishness of superstitions. However, public opinion was against him and in favor of Long Jack, who told the most terrifying ghost stories till midnight. Normally, the men accused the cook about "idolatry" whenever he performed one of his mysterious rituals to keep away bad spirits. But on this night, the men were so spooked that no one said a word when he floated a candle in water to keep the dead

Frenchman quiet. Dan lit the candle because he had bought the knife belt, and the cook muttered prayers and chants until the flickering candle burned out.

As they went to bed after watch, Harvey asked Dan, "What about progress and Catholic superstitions?"

"Huh! I guess I'm as enlightened and progressive as the next man. But when it comes to a dead St. Malo fisherman scarin' a couple o' poor boys stiff fer the sake of a thirty-cent knife, well, then, the cook can light every candle in the world."

The next morning, all the men were rather ashamed of the previous night's ceremonies—all, except the cook. They went to work immediately, and spoke roughly to one another.

The *We're Here* was racing neck and neck against the *Parry Norman* for her last few loads of fish. The struggle was so close that the fleet took sides and bet tobacco. All hands worked at fishing or dressing-down until they fell asleep where they stood. They even had the cook help with pitching the fish, and put Harvey in the hold to pass salt while Dan helped to dress down. Luckily, a Parry Norman man sprained his ankle and the *We're Here* took the lead. Harvey could not see how one more fish could be crammed into her, but Disko and Tom Platt stowed and stowed. They flattened the piles of fish with big stones, and there was always "jest one more day's work." Disko did not tell them when the hold was finally full. He simply walked to the front storage hold and began hauling out the huge main sail, which would carry them home. This was at ten in the morning. The main sail was up by noon, and dories came alongside with letters for the men to take back home, envying their good fortune. At last she hoisted her flag, as is the right of the first boat off the Banks, pulled up her anchor, and began to move. Disko worked the *We're Here* gracefully in and out among the schooners. It was his little parade of victory, and for the fifth year running it showed what kind of mariner he was. Dan's accordion and Tom Platt's fiddle supplied the music of the magic verse you must not sing till the ship has filled its storage hold:

> Hi! Hi! Yoho! Send your letters round!
> All our salt is wetted, an' the anchor's off the ground!
> Bend, oh, bend your main sail, we're back to Yankeeland
> With fifteen thousand pounds,
> And fifteen thousand pounds,
> And fifteen thousand pounds,
> 'Tween old Gloucester an' Grand!

The last letters were tossed on deck wrapped around pieces of coal. The Gloucester men shouted messages to their wives and children, while the *We're Here* finished its musical ride through the fleet. Her sails quivering like a man's hand waving goodbye.

Harvey soon discovered that the *We're Here* was a very different ship with her main sail up. Her sails flattened against the wind like a racing yacht, and the streaming line of bubbles alongside made his eyes dizzy.

Disko kept them busy fiddling with the sails or pumping out the water that collected at the bottom of the fish piles. But since there was no fishing, Harvey had time to look at the sea from another point of view. The ship seemed to elbow, fidget and coast her way through the gray foaming waves. Or, she would rub herself like a cat along the side of the larger waterhills. It was as if she said: "You wouldn't hurt me, would you? I'm only the little *We're Here*." Then she would slide away, chuckling softly to herself till she was confronted by some fresh obstacle. Harvey began to understand the ocean. He enjoyed the chorus of crashing waves, and the hurried winds that swept across the sea and herded the purple-blue clouds. He loved the wonderful red sunrise and the way the morning mists would melt away in the sun, the salty glare of noon, the kiss of rain falling over thousands of flat ocean miles, the chilly black of dusk, and the million wrinkles of the sea under moonlight.

They left the cold gray of the Bank sea and

made their way west. They saw the lumber ships making for Quebec, Canada, and picked up a friendly storm that blew them past Sable Island and stayed with them to the northern edge of George's Island off the coast of Boston. From there they picked up the deeper water and let her go merrily.

"Hattie's waitin' on me," Dan confided to Harvey. "Hattie an' Ma. Next Sunday you'll be hirin' a boy to throw water on the windows to make ye go to sleep. 'Guess you'll stay with us till your folks come. Do you know the best part of gettin' ashore again?"

"Hot bath?" said Harvey. His eyebrows were all white with dried salt spray.

"That's good, but pajamas are better. I've been dreamin' of clean pajamas fer months. Ma'll hev a new set fer me, all washed soft. It's home, Harve. It's home! Ye can sense it in the air. Wonder if we'll get home in time fer supper."

The sails flapped as the blue sea smoothed out around them. Then came the rain in spiky droplets, and behind the rain, the thunder and the lightning of mid-August. They lay on the deck with bare feet and arms, telling one another what they would order at their first meal ashore. Land was now in plain sight. A Gloucester swordfish boat drifted alongside, and a man hollered to them. "And all's well!" he sang cheerily. "Wouverman's waiting fer you, Disko. What's the news o' the fleet?"

Disko shouted it and sailed on, while the wild summer storm pounded overhead and finally died down. The *We're Here* crawled along the coast. Under the twinkling stars and moonlight, Harvey could make out the low hills and houses around Gloucester Harbor.

"The flag, the flag!" said Disko, suddenly, pointing upward.

"What is it?" said Long Jack.

"For Otto! Set the flag at half mast. They can see us from shore now."

"I'd clean forgot. He's no family in Gloucester, has he?"

"Girl he was goin' to be married to this fall."

"Mary pity her!" said Long Jack, and lowered the little flag half-mast for the sake of Otto, swept overboard in a storm three months before.

Disko wiped the wet from his eyes and led the *We're Here* to Wouverman's pier. Harvey could feel the land close round him once more, with all its thousands of people asleep, and the smell of earth after rain. All these things made his heart beat and his throat dry up as he stood on deck. They slipped into a pocket of darkness where a lantern glimmered on either side. Somebody awoke with a grunt, threw them a rope, and they tied the ship to a silent pier and lay there without a sound.

Then Harvey sat down by the wheel, and

sobbed and sobbed as though his heart would break. A tall woman who had been sitting on a weigh scale dropped down into the schooner and kissed Dan once on the cheek. She was his mother, and she had seen the *We're Here* by the lightning flashes. She took no notice of Harvey till he had recovered himself a little and Disko had told her his story. Then they went to Disko's house together as the dawn was breaking; and until the telegraph office was open and he could wire his folks, Harvey Cheyne was perhaps the loneliest boy in all America. But the curious thing was that Disko and Dan did not think less of him for crying.

Wouverman was not happy with Disko's prices. But Disko was sure that the *We're Here* was at least a week ahead of any other Gloucester boat, so he gave Wouverman a few days to think about it. Meanwhile, the men relaxed, played about the streets and enjoyed themselves. But Dan walked about with his freckled nose in the air, acting quite secretive and stuck-up to his family.

"Dan, I'll hev to lay into you ef you act this way," said Troop. "Since we've come ashore this time, you've bin a heap too fresh."

"I'd lay into him now if he was mine," said Uncle Salters, sourly. He and Penn stayed with the Troops.

Disko was smoking a cigar in all his onshore glory in a pair of beautiful slippers. You're gettin' as crazy as poor Harve. You two go around gigglin' an' whisperin' and kickin' each other under the table till there's no peace in the house," he said.

"There's goin' to be a heap less peace—fer some folks," Dan replied. "You wait an' see."

He and Harvey went out on the trolley to East Gloucester, where they ran to the lighthouse, sat down on the big red boulders and laughed themselves hungry. Harvey had shown Dan a telegram, and the two swore to keep silent till the secret was out.

"Harve's parents?" said Dan, with a blank face after supper. "Well, I guess they don't amount to much of anything, or we'd ha' heard from 'em by now. His pop works at a store out West. Maybe he'll give you as much as five dollars, Dad."

"What did I tell ye?" said Salters. "Don't talk while yer eating, Dan."

CHAPTER 9

Like any other working man, a multimillionaire should stay on top of his business, no matter what his private sorrows may be. Harvey Cheyne, Sr. had gone east late in June to meet his devastated wife, who dreamed day and night about her son drowning in the gray seas. He had surrounded her with doctors, trained nurses and even spiritual healers, but they were all useless. Mrs. Cheyne lay still and moaned, or talked about her son to anyone who would listen. She had no hope of finding him alive.

All she wanted was assurance that drowning did not hurt, and her husband stood guard in case she decided to find out herself. He did not say much about his own sorrow. He hardly realized how grief-stricken he was, until he caught himself asking the calendar on his writing desk, "What's the use of going on?"

In the back of his mind, he had always had an idea that, some day, when the boy had finished college, he would take him under his wing and teach him the family business. Then, he argued (as busy fathers do), the boy would instantly become his companion, partner, and ally. Wonderful years would follow, filled with great accomplishments by father and son. Now his boy was dead—lost at sea. His wife was dying from grief, and he himself was plagued by platoons of doctors and maids and attendants. He was sick with worry over her poor, restless state, with no energy to meet his many enemies.

He had taken his wife to his new mansion in San Diego, where she and her people occupied a tremendous wing. Cheyne toiled from day to day in a small office between a secretary and a typist, who also worked the telegram machine. There was a war over ticket prices among four western railroads, in which he was supposed to be interested. A devastating strike had developed in his lumber camps in Oregon, and the California legislature was preparing open war against him.

Ordinarily, he would have accepted battle wherever it was offered, and waged a ruthless campaign in response. But now he sat limply, his soft black hat pushed forward on to his nose, his big body shrunk inside his loose clothes. He stared at his boots, and nodded absently to the secretary's questions as he opened the Saturday mail. Cheyne was wondering how much it would cost to drop everything and pull out. He could move to one of his homes in Colorado and forget his future plans that had come to nothing.

Suddenly, the click of the typewriter stopped. The girl was looking at the secretary, who had turned white. He passed Cheyne a telegram, which read:

> Picked up by fishing schooner We're Here having fallen off boat. Great times fishing on Banks. All is well. Waiting in Gloucester Mass., care of Disko Troop. How is Mama? Harvey N. Cheyne.

The father let it fall, laid his head down on the top of the shut desk, and breathed heavily. The secretary ran for Mrs. Cheyne's doctor, who found Cheyne pacing to and fro.

"What—what d' you think of it? Is it possible? Is there any meaning to it? I can't quite understand it," he cried.

"I can," said the doctor. "It says I'm about to lose seven thousand dollars a year—that's all." He thought of the struggling New York practice he had abandoned at Cheyne's bossy request. He returned the telegram with a sigh.

"Should we tell her? Maybe it's a fake?"

"What's the motive?" said the doctor, coolly. "It's the boy, sure enough."

A maid entered the room. "Mrs. Cheyne says you must come at once. She thinks you are sick."

The master of thirty millions bowed his head meekly and followed Suzanne. A thin, high voice echoed from the top of the grand white-wood staircase. "What is it? What has happened?"

No doors could keep out the shriek that rang through the house a moment later, when her husband blurted out the news.

"Milsom, we're going right across. Private car—straight through to Boston. Make the arrangements," shouted Cheyne down the staircase.

The secretary turned to the typist. He motioned to her to move to the telegram machine like a general commanding his troops. Then he got to work, pouring over the train schedules and deciding which route would be fastest. Meanwhile, Miss Kinzey's white fingers called up the Continent of America.

"Cheyne's private train car, the *Constance*, is in Los Angeles, isn't she, Miss Kinzey?"

"Yep." Miss Kinzey nodded between clicks of Morse code as the secretary looked at his watch.

"Ready? Send private car *Constance* and arrange to leave Sunday in time to connect with the *New York Limited* at Sixteenth Street, Chicago, next Tuesday."

Click-lick-lick, went the telegraph.

"Also arrange to take *Constance* on the *New York Central* from New York City to Boston. Of great importance, I should reach Boston Wednesday evening. Be sure nothing prevents. Have also wired Canniff, Toucey, and Barnes. Signed, Cheyne."

Miss Kinzey nodded, and the secretary went on.

"Now then. Canniff, Toucey, and Barnes, of course. Ready? Canniff, Chicago. Please take my private car *Constance* from the "Santa Fe" train at Sixteenth Street next Tuesday p.m. Transfer to *New York Limited* and deliver N.Y.C. for Albany. Take car Buffalo to Albany on *Limited* Tuesday p.m. That's for Toucey."

"Now, Boston and Albany, Barnes, same instructions from Albany through to Boston. Leave three P. M., arrive nine P. M. Wednesday. That covers everything."

"It's great," said Miss Kinzey, with a look of admiration. "But see here, about that *New York Limited*. The president himself couldn't hitch his private car to that train," Miss Kinzey suggested.

"Yes, but this isn't the president. It's Cheyne," responded the secretary.

"Guess we'd better wire the boy. You've forgotten that."

"I'll ask."

He returned with the father's message, which instructed Harvey to meet them in Boston. He found Miss Kinzey laughing over the telegram machine. Then Milsom laughed, too, when he read the frantic messages from Los Angeles: "We want to know why-why-why? General uneasiness developed and spreading."

Ten minutes later Chicago appealed to Miss

Kinzey in these words: "If crime of century is developing, please warn friends in time. We are all taking cover here."

This was topped by a message from Topeka (and why Topeka was concerned, even Milsom could not guess): "Don't shoot, Colonel. We'll compromise on ticket rates."

When he saw the telegrams, Cheyne smiled at the anxiety of his enemies. "They think we're on the warpath. Tell 'em we don't feel like fighting right now, Milsom. Tell 'em what we're going for. I guess you and Miss Kinzey had better come along, though I doubt I will do any business on the road. Tell 'em the truth—for once."

So the truth was told. Miss Kinzey relayed the story while the secretary added the memorable quotation, "Let us have peace." In board rooms two thousand miles away, the representatives of sixty-three million dollars' worth of railroad interests breathed a sigh of relief. Cheyne was rushing to meet his only son, who had been miraculously restored to him. The bear was seeking his cub, not the bulls. Hard men who had their knives drawn to fight for their financial lives put away the weapons and wished him God-speed.

It was a busy weekend on the telegraph wires. Now that their anxiety was relieved, men and cities rushed to accommodate Cheyne's cross-country trip. The magnificent *Constance*,

Cheyne's private train car, along with an engineer and full staff, would be rushed over those two thousand three hundred and fifty miles. The car would be attached and then transferred from train to train, and take priority over one hundred and seventy-seven others cars that wished to do the same. Dispatchers and crews of every one of those trains must be notified. Sixteen locomotives, sixteen engineers, and sixteen firemen would be needed—each and every one the best available. Two and one half minutes would be allowed for changing trains. "Warn the men, and make every arrangement, for Harvey Cheyne is in a hurry, a hurry, a hurry," sang the telegraph wires. "Forty miles an hour will be expected. From San Diego to Sixteenth Street, Chicago, lay down the magic carpet. Hurry! Oh, hurry!"

"It will be hot," said Cheyne, as they rolled

out of San Diego in the dawn of Sunday. "We're going to hurry, Mama, just as fast as we can. But I really do think it's too early to put on your hat and gloves. You should lie down and take your medicine."

"I'll be fine. Oh, I will be fine. Only—taking off my hat makes me feel like we'll never get there."

"Try to sleep a little, Mama, and we'll be in Chicago before you know it."

"Tell them to hurry."

The train hammered its way through the Mojave Desert. The heat of the desert was followed by the heat of the hills as they turned east towards the Colorado River. The car sweltered in the utter drought and glare. They put crushed ice on Mrs. Cheyne's neck, and toiled up the long, steep mountains towards Flagstaff, Arizona and its dry, empty sky. The crew of the *Constance* sat in their bunks, panting in their shirtsleeves. Cheyne found himself among them, shouting old railroad stories that every trainman already knew, above the roar of the car. He told them about his son, and how the sea had given up its dead, and they nodded and spit and rejoiced with him.

But Mrs. Cheyne, who lay in the master sleeping cabin, only moaned a little and begged her husband to "hurry." And so they dropped the dry sands of Arizona behind them, and pushed on till the squeal of the brakes told them they were in New Mexico. From there, they sped past Albuquerque, caught sight of Arkansas and tore down the long slope to Dodge City, Kansas, where Cheyne took comfort from setting his watch an hour ahead.

There was very little talk in the car. The secretary and typist sat together on the Spanish leather cushions by the plate glass observation window at the rear of the car. Cheyne walked nervously from one end to the other, an unlit cigar in his teeth. He was so distraught that the pitying crewmen forgot he was rich, and therefore their tribal enemy, and did their best to entertain him.

At Dodge City, an unknown person threw in a copy of a Kansas paper containing an interview with Harvey. The joyful article confirmed that it was their boy, and it soothed Mrs. Cheyne for a while. Her one word "hurry" was conveyed by the crews to the engineers at Topeka, and Marceline, Missouri, where the earth flattened out and they picked up speed. Towns and villages were close together now, and they could feel that they were making progress.

"I can't see the odometer, and my eyes ache so. How are we doing?"

"The very best we can, Mama. There's no sense in getting in before the *New York Limited*. We'd only have to wait."

"I don't care. I want to feel we're moving. Sit

down and tell me the miles."

Cheyne sat down and read the mileage from the train's odometer for her, but the seventy-foot car never changed its long steamer-like roll. It moved through the heat with the hum of a giant bee. Yet the speed was not enough for Mrs. Cheyne, and the August heat was making her queasy. The clock hands would not move, and when, oh, when would they be in Chicago?

They changed tracks at Fort Madison, Iowa, and finally reached Chicago, where the *Limited* whirled the *Constance* into New York City and finally, into Boston. The trip from ocean to ocean took eighty-seven hours and thirty-five minutes, or three days, fifteen and a half hours. Harvey was waiting for them.

After violent emotion and upset, most people and all boys demand food. The Cheyne family feasted behind drawn curtains, in a private bubble of great happiness, while the trains roared in and out around them. Harvey ate, drank, and detailed his adventures all in one breath, and when he had a hand free his mother held it. His voice was deeper from living in the open, salt air; his palms were rough and hard, and a fine full scent of codfish hung round his rubber boots and blue jersey.

The father, who was used to judging men, looked at Harvey carefully. He caught himself thinking that he knew very little about his son.

However, he clearly remembered a spoiled, pale-faced youth who took delight in making his mother cry. But this young fisherman did not squirm like a young boy and looked at him with steady, clear, and unflinching eyes. He spoke to his parents in a very respectful way, and his parents got the impression that the change might be permanent, and the new Harvey had come to stay.

"Someone's been disciplining him," thought Cheyne. "Now my wife would never have allowed that. Don't think Europe could have done it any better."

"But why didn't you tell this man, Troop, who you were?" the mother repeated, when Harvey had told his story at least twice.

"Disko Troop. The best man that ever walked a deck."

"Why didn't you tell him to bring you ashore? You know your father would have made it up to him ten times over."

"I know, but he thought I was crazy. I'm afraid I called him a thief because I couldn't find the money in my pocket."

"A sailor found it on deck that—that night," sobbed Mrs. Cheyne.

"That explains it, then. I don't blame Troop any. I just said I wouldn't work on a Bank schooner—and of course he hit me on the nose, and oh! I bled like a stuck hog."

"My poor darling! They must have abused you horribly."

"Nah. After that, I saw a light."

Cheyne slapped his leg and chuckled. This was going to be a boy after his own hungry heart. He had never seen that twinkle in Harvey's eye before.

"And the old man gave me ten and a half dollars a month. He's paid me half already. I partnered with Dan and pitched right in. I can't do a man's work yet. But I can handle a dory almost as well as Dan, and I don't get scared in a fog— much, and I can bait up a trawl line, and I know my ropes, of course, and I can pitch fish till the cows come home. Say, you've no idea how much work there is in ten and a half a month!"

"I began with eight and a half, my son," said Cheyne.

"That so? You never told me, sir."

"You never asked, Harve. I'll tell you about it some day, if you care to listen. Have a stuffed olive."

"It's great to have a meal like this again. We were well fed, though. Disko fed us first-class. He's a great man. And Dan—that's his son— Dan's my partner. And there's Uncle Salters and his manures. He's sure I'm crazy. And there's poor little Penn, and he really is crazy. You mustn't talk to him about Johnstown, because . . ."

"And, oh, you must know Tom Platt and Long Jack and Manuel. Manuel saved my life.

He's Portuguese. He can't talk much, but he's a wonderful musician. He found me and hauled me in."

"I'm amazed that your nervous system isn't completely wrecked," said Mrs. Cheyne.

"What for, Mama? I worked like a horse and I ate like a hog and I slept like a dead man."

That was too much for Mrs. Cheyne, who began to think of her dreams of a corpse rocking on the salty seas. She went to her stateroom, and Harvey curled up beside his father, explaining his gratitude to the men of the *We're Here*.

"You can count on me to do everything I can for the crowd, Harve. They sound like good men."

"Best in the fleet, sir. Ask anyone in Gloucester," said Harvey. "But Disko still believes he's cured me of being crazy. Dan's the only one I told about you, and our private cars and all the rest of it, and I'm not quite sure Dan even believes me. I want to surprise 'em tomorrow. Say, can't they run the *Constance* over to Gloucester? Mama don't look fit to be moved, anyway, and we're bound to finish cleaning out the ship by tomorrow. Wouverman bought our fish. You see, we're the first off the Banks this season, so we get to set our price. We held out till he paid it."

"You mean you'll have to work tomorrow?"

"I told Troop I would. I'm on the scales. I've

brought the tallies with me." He looked at the greasy notebook with an air of importance that made his father choke.

"Hire a substitute," suggested Cheyne, to see what Harvey would say.

"Can't, sir. I'm tally man for the schooner. Troop says I've a better head for numbers than Dan. Troop's a mighty fair man."

"Well, suppose I don't move the *Constance* tonight. What'll you do then?"

Harvey looked at the clock, which said twenty past eleven.

"Then I'll sleep here till three and catch the four o'clock freight train. They let us men from the fleet ride for free."

"That's an idea. But I think we can get the *Constance* there faster than your men's freight train. Better go to bed now."

Harvey spread himself on the sofa, kicked off his boots, and was asleep before his father could pull down the shades. Cheyne sat watching his son's young face, and it occurred to him that he might have been a neglectful father.

"You never know when you're taking the biggest risks," he said to himself. "Growing up without a father, that might have been worse than drowning. I haven't enough money to pay Disko Troop for what he's done."

Morning brought a fresh sea breeze through the windows. The *Constance* was stuck among the freight cars at Gloucester, so Harvey had gone ahead to his business.

"He'll fall overboard again and be drowned," the mother said bitterly.

"We'll go and watch him, ready to throw him a rope just in case. You've never seen him working for his bread," said the father.

"What nonsense! As if anyone expected—"

"Well, the man that hired him did. He's absolutely right, too."

They went down between the stores full of fishermen's oilskins to Wouverman's wharf where the *We're Here* rode high, her Bank flag still flying. All hands busy as beavers in the glorious morning light. Disko stood by the main hatch supervising Manuel, Penn and Uncle Salters down below. Dan was swinging the loaded baskets onto the dock as Long Jack and Tom Platt filled them. Harvey, with a notebook, represented the skipper's interests before the clerk of the scales on the salt-sprinkled pier.

"Ready!" cried the voices below. "Haul!" cried Disko. "Hi!" said Manuel. "Here!" said Dan, swinging the basket. Then they heard Harvey's voice, clear and fresh, checking the weights.

The last of the fish had been whipped out, and Harvey leaped on deck to hand Disko the tally, shouting, "Two ninety-seven, and an empty hold!"

"What's the total, Harve?" said Disko.

"Eight sixty-five. Three thousand six hundred and seventy-six dollars and a quarter. Wish I had a share o' the boat as well as my wage."

"Well, I won't say you hevn't earned it, Harve. Don't you want to slip up to Wouverman's office and take him our tallies?"

"Who's that boy?" said Cheyne to Dan, who was used to all sorts of question from those wealthy, lazy imbeciles who vacationed in Gloucester.

"Well, he's kind of our supercargo," was the answer. "We picked him up drifting on the Banks. Fell overboard from a passenger ship, he sez. He was a passenger. He's a fisherman now, though."

"Is he worth his keep?"

"Ye-ep. Dad, this man wants to know ef Harve's worth his keep! Say, would you like to come aboard? We'll fix up a ladder for you."

"I should very much, indeed. 'Twon't hurt you, Mama, and you'll be able to see for yourself."

The woman who could not lift her head a week ago scrambled down the ladder, and stood horrified amid the mess and tangle of ropes.

"You're interested in Harve?" asked Disko.

"Well, ye-es."

"He's a good boy, an' does what he's told. You've heard how we found him? He was sufferin' from shock, I guess, or else his head hit somethin' when we hauled him aboard. He's all over that now. Yes, this is the cabin. 'Tain't cleaned up yet, but you're quite welcome to look around. Those are his figures on the stovepipe, where we record our latitude an' longitude.

"Did he sleep here?" said Mrs. Cheyne, sitting on a yellow locker and surveying the disorderly bunks.

"Yes. And except for him an' my boy sneakin' fried pies an staying up when they ought to ha' been asleep, I can't find any special fault with him."

"There weren't nothin' wrong with Harve," said Uncle Salters, descending the steps. "He hung my boots on the main mast, and he ain't much respectful to them who knows more'n he do, specially about farmin'; but he was mostly misled by Dan on that subject."

In the meantime, Dan was performing a war dance on deck. "Tom, Tom!" he whispered down the hatch. "His folks has come, an' Dad ain't caught on yet. They're conversin' in the cabin. She's a beauty, an' he's all Harve claimed he was, by the looks of him."

"Holy smoke!" said Long Jack, climbing out covered with salt and fish skin. "D'ye think his tale uv the kid an' the little four-horse carriage was true?"

"I knew it all along," said Dan. "Come an' see Dad mistook in his judgments."

They came delightedly, just in time to hear Cheyne say: "I'm glad he has a good character, because—he's my son."

Disko's jaw fell—Long Jack always swore that he actually heard the click of it—and he stared at the man and the woman.

"I got his telegram in San Diego four days ago, and we came over."

"In a private car?" said Dan. "He said ye might."

"In a private car, of course."

Dan looked at his father with a flurry of winks.

"There was a tale he told us uv drivin' four little ponies in a carriage uv his own," said Long Jack. "Was that true?"

"Probably," said Cheyne. "Was it, Mama?"

"He had a little carriage when we were in Toledo, I think," said the mother.

Long Jack whistled. "Oh, Disko!" said he, and that was all.

"I wuz—I am mistook in my judgments," said Disko, as though the words were being whipped out of him. "I don't mind tellin' you the truth, Mr. Cheyne. I suspected the boy to be crazy. He talked kind of odd about money."

"So he told me."

"Did he tell ye anything else? 'Cause I pounded him once." This was said with a somewhat anxious glance at Mrs. Cheyne.

"Oh, yes," Cheyne replied. "It probably did him more good than anything else in the world."

"I judged it wuz necessary, or I wouldn't ha' done it. I don't want you to think we abuse our boys any on this ship."

"I don't think you do, Mr. Troop."

Mrs. Cheyne had been looking at the faces—Disko's iron features, Penn's bewildered simplicity, Manuel's quiet smile, Long Jack's grin of delight, and Tom Platt's scar. They were certainly rough by her standards, but she had a mother's intuition in her eyes and she rose with outstretched hands.

"Oh, tell me, who is who?" said she, half sobbing. "I want to thank you and bless you—all of you."

Disko introduced each of the men, and Mrs. Cheyne babbled incoherently. She nearly threw herself into Manuel's arms when she understood that he had first found Harvey.

"But how shall I leave him adrift?" said poor Manuel. "What would you do if you find him so? We found us one good boy, and I am ever so pleased he come to be your son."

"And he told me Dan was his partner!" she cried. Dan was already sufficiently pink, but he turned a rich red when Mrs. Cheyne kissed him on both cheeks. Then they led her to the kitchen, where she wept again. There she found the cook cleaning up the stove, and he nodded as though she were someone he had expected to meet for years. They tried, two at a time, to explain the boat's daily life to her, and she sat at the table, her gloved hands on the greasy surface, laughing with trembling lips and crying with dancing eyes.

"Who can use the *We're Here* after this?" said Long Jack to Tom Platt. "I feel as if she's made it a cathedral."

"Then Harvey was not crazy," said Penn, slowly, to Cheyne.

"No, indeed—thank God," the big millionaire replied, stooping down tenderly.

"It must be terrible to be crazy. But to lose your child—I do not know anything more terrible. Your child has come back? Let us thank God for that."

"Hello!" cried Harvey, looking down upon them casually from the pier.

"I wuz mistook, Harve. I wuz mistook," said Disko quickly, holding up a hand. "I wuz mistook in my judgments. Ye needn't rub it in anymore."

"Guess I'll take care o' that," said Dan, under his breath.

"You'll be headed home now, won't ye?"

"Well, not without the balance of my wages."

"I clean forgot," and Disko counted out the remaining dollars. "You done all you promised to do, Harve, and you done it 'bout as well as if you'd been brought up . . ." Here Disko stopped himself. He did not quite see where the sentence was going to end.

"Outside of a private car?" suggested Dan, with a wink.

"Come on, and I'll show her to you," said Harvey.

Cheyne stayed to talk with Disko, but the others made a procession to the train station. Harvey let the *Constance* speak for herself, and the men looked around silently at the leather seats, silver door handles, velvet blankets and rare wood furniture.

"I told you," said Harvey, "I told you." This was his crowning revenge.

Mrs. Cheyne ordered a meal, and as Long Jack pointed out with amazement every time he told the story afterwards, she waited on them herself. Men who are accustomed to eating at tiny tables in howling sea storms have extremely neat table manners. Mrs. Cheyne, who did not know this, was astounded. She was impressed by the way Manuel moved so silently and easily among the fragile glassware and dainty silver. Tom Platt remembered the great days on the *Ohio* and the manners of foreign dignitaries who dined with the officers. And Long Jack, being Irish, supplied the small talk till everyone felt comfortable and happy.

In the cabin of the *We're Here*, the fathers took stock of each other behind their cigars.

Cheyne knew well enough when he dealt with a man to whom he could not offer money. He also knew that no money could pay for what Disko had done.

"I hevn't done anything to your boy or fer your boy excep' make him work an' teach him how to handle the hog yoke," said Disko. "He has twice my boy's head for figures."

"By the way," Cheyne answered casually, "what do you plan to make of your boy?"

Disko removed his cigar and waved it around the cabin. "Dan's jest a plain boy, an' he don't allow me to do any of his thinkin'. He'll hev this able little ship when I'm too old to be at sea. He ain't noways anxious to quit the fishing business. I know that."

"Mmm! 'Ever been West, Mr. Troop?"

"'Bin's far ez Noo York once in a boat. I've no use for railroads. Neither has Dan. Salt water's good enough fer the Troops."

"I can give him all the salt water he's likely to need—till he's a skipper."

"How's that? I thought you wuz some kinder railroad king. Harve told me so when—I was mistook in my judgments."

"We all make mistakes. I also own a line of tea ships—San Francisco to Yokohama, Japan—six of 'em, iron-built, about seventeen hundred and eighty tons apiece.

"Blame that boy! He never told me. I'd ha'

listened to that, instead o' his goin' on about rail-roads an' pony carriages."

"He didn't know."

"Little thing like that slipped his mind, I guess."

"No, I only took over the Blue M. Shipping Company—Morgan and McQuade's old fleet—this summer." Disko collapsed where he sat beside the stove.

"Great Caesar Almighty! I've been fooled from one end to the other. Why, Phil Airheart, he went from this very town six year back—no, seven—an' he works on the freighter called "San Jose" now. And you now own the Blue M. freighters?"

Cheyne nodded.

"If I'd known that, I'd ha' jerked the *We're Here* back to port right away."

"Perhaps that wouldn't have been so good for Harvey."

"If I'd only known! If he'd only mentioned the cussed freighters, I'd ha' understood! I'll never stand on my own judgments again—never. They're well-made ships. Phil Airheart he says so."

"Airheart's skipper of the San Jose now. Would you lend me Dan for a year or two, and we'll see if we can't make a sailor of him? Would you trust him to Airheart?"

"It's a risk taking a young boy—"

"I know a man who did more for me."

"That's diff'runt. Look here now, I ain't rec-ommendin' Dan special because he's my own flesh an' blood. I know Bank schooners ain't same as tea ships, but he ain't got much to learn. He can steer a ship better than most men. The rest is in our blood, but I do wish he warn't so blame weak on navigation."

"Airheart will teach him. Suppose he stays here through winter, and I'll send for him early in the spring. I know the Pacific's a long ways off—"

"I ain't worried 'bout that! We Troops, livin' an' dead, are all around the earth an' seas."

"But I want you to understand—and I mean this—any time you think you'd like to see him, tell me, and I'll take care of the transportation. It won't cost you a cent."

"If you'll walk with me, we'll go to my house an' talk about this with my wife. I've bin so crazy mistook in all my judgments, none of this seems real."

They walked over to Troop's beautiful white house, with an old dory displayed in the front yard and a sitting room which was filled with unusual gifts from overseas. There sat a large woman. She was silent and sad, with the tired eyes of someone who has waited a long time for her loved ones to return. Cheyne spoke with her, and she agreed to his plan with a heavy sigh.

"We lose one hundred men a year from Gloucester alone, Mr. Cheyne," she said. "One hundred boys an' men. I've come to hate the sea as if it was alive and listening. God never meant for humans to anchor on the sea. These ships of yours, they go straight to Japan, and straight home again?"

"As straight as the winds let 'em, and I give a bonus for record-fast passages. Tea don't improve by being at sea."

"When Dan wuz little he used to pretend he was a store owner. I hoped he might follow that path. But soon as he could paddle a dory I knew he'd be at sea like his father."

"The tea ships are square-riggers, Mother; iron-built an' strong as anything."

"If Dan agrees, Mr. Cheyne, he can go, I suppose."

"She just despises the ocean," Disko explained, "an' I—I don't know how to act polite, I guess, or I'd thank you better."

"My father, my own eldest brother, two nephews, an' my sister's husband," she said, dropping her head on her hand. "They were all killed at sea. Wouldn't you despise something that took away these men?"

Cheyne was relieved when Dan turned up and accepted with more excitement than he was able to put into words. Indeed, the offer meant a plain and sure road to success and a bright future. But Dan was most excited about the idea of standing watch on huge decks, and looking into faraway harbors.

Privately, Mrs. Cheyne had spoken to kind-hearted Manuel about Harvey's rescue. He seemed to have no interest in money. When she insisted, he said that he would take five dollars because he wanted to buy something for a girl. Otherwise, he said, "How shall I take money when I make good wages and pay easy for my food and smokes? Will you give some to the church if I say?" He introduced her to a Portuguese priest who had a long list of poor widows in need. Mrs. Cheyne gave an impressive donation to the priest, while Manuel headed to town to get a handkerchief for the girl. Mrs. Cheyne watched him as he left, and felt a great amount of respect for the sweet and kind Manuel.

Salters headed west with Penn, and left no address behind. He was afraid that these million-aire people, with their wasteful private cars, might take an unwanted interest in Penn. It was better to visit relatives till the coast was clear. "Never git adopted by rich folk, Penn," he said as they traveled, "or I'll break this checkerboard over your head. If you forget your name again— which is Pratt—you remember you belong with Salters Troop, an' sit down right where you are till I come fer you. Never follow folks whose eyes are fat with greed, as scripture says."

CHAPTER 10

It was different with the *We're Here*'s silent cook, who came up from the kitchen and promptly boarded the *Constance*. His purpose, as revealed to him in dreams, was to follow Harvey for the rest of his days. He did not want money, and he didn't care where he slept. They tried to argue with him, but the cook would not be swayed. Cheyne presumed that Harvey might need a cook some day, and was sure that one volunteer was worth five hired men. The *Constance* would go back to Boston, where, if the cook still insisted, they would take him West and look after him, just as he planned to look after Harvey.

With the *Constance* waiting in Boston, Cheyne decided to learn more about Gloucester. This was a new town in a new land for the millionaire, and he decided to "take it in" as he had done with all the cities from Chicago to San Diego. He and Harvey strolled along the streets of Gloucester, which were filled with piers and ship supply stores. As a businessman, he wanted to learn how the fishing business worked. The townsmen told Cheyne that four out of every five fish dinners served at New England's dinner tables came from Gloucester, and overwhelmed him with proof—statistics of boats, fishing gear, the number of piers, salting, packing, factories, insurance, wages, repairs, and profits. He talked with the owners of the large fleets whose captains were little more than hired men, and whose crews were almost all Swedish or Portuguese. Then he consulted with Disko, one of the few men who owned their own fishing vessel, and compared notes in his head. He barged into the insurance company offices, and demanded explanations of how the whole business worked. He spent hours in the marine junkyards, asking questions with cheerful curiosity, until the entire town wanted to know "what in thunder that man was after, anyhow."

Meanwhile, Mrs. Cheyne rested in a small boarding house nearby. The place was filled with summer vacationers, mostly from Boston. They were not wealthy folks by Mrs. Cheyne's standards.

"But they are most delightful people," she confided to her husband, "so friendly and simple, too."

"That isn't simplicity, Mama," he said, looking across the boulders behind the apple trees where the hammocks were slung. "It's something else—something I don't possess."

"How can that be?" said Mrs. Cheyne quietly. "There isn't a woman here who owns a dress worth more than a hundred dollars. Why, we—"

"I know it, dear. We have everything—of course we have. Are you having a good time?"

"I don't see very much of Harvey. He's always with you. But I'm not nearly as nervous as I was."

"I can't remember when I've had such a good time. I never really understood that I had a son before this. Harve's a great boy. Anything I can fetch you, dear? Cushion under your head? Well, we'll go down to the water again and look around."

Harvey was his father's shadow in those days, and the two strolled along side by side. Cheyne used the steep hills as an excuse for laying his hand on the boy's square shoulder. It was then that Harvey noticed and admired what had never struck him before. His father had an amazing ability to learn something new from the roughest, and most uneducated, men he encountered.

"How d'you make 'em tell you everything?" demanded the son, as they came out of a schooner's cabin.

"I've dealt with quite a few men in my time, Harve, and I've learned how to size 'em up somehow, I guess. I know something about myself, too." Then, after a pause, as they sat down on the edge of a pier, "Men can 'most always tell when a man has handled things for himself, and then they treat him as one of their own."

"Same as they treat me down at Wouverman's pier. I'm one of the crowd now. Disko's told everyone I've earned my pay." Harvey spread out his hands and rubbed the palms together. "They're all soft again," he said sadly.

"Keep 'em that way for the next few years, while you're getting your education. You can harden 'em up afterwards."

"Ye-es, I suppose so," was the unhappy reply.

"It's up to you, Harve. You can hide behind your mama, of course, and have her worry again about your nerves and your demands and all that kind of rubbish."

"Have I ever done that?" said Harvey, uneasily.

His father turned and looked at his son. "You know as well as I do that I can't make anything of you if you don't act straight with me. I can handle you alone if you'll stay alone, but I won't put up with the nonsense you gave your mother. Life's too short, anyway."

"Don't make me much of a fellow, does it?"

"I guess it was partially my fault. But if you want the truth, you haven't been much of anything up to now, have you?"

"Say, what d'you think it's cost you to raise me?"

Cheyne smiled. "I've never kept track. But if I had to guess, close to sixty thousand dollars. The young generation comes at a high price. It has to have new things, and it tires of 'em quickly, and the old man foots the bill."

Harvey whistled, but secretly, he was rather pleased to think that his upbringing had cost so much. "And all that money's wasted, isn't it?"

"Invested, Harve. Invested, I hope."

"I've only earned thirty dollars. That's a mighty poor investment." Harvey shook his head solemnly.

Cheyne laughed till he nearly fell off the pier into the water.

"Disko has got a heap more than that out of Dan since he was ten, and Dan's at school half the year, too."

"Oh, that's what you're after, is it? To only go to school for half the year?"

"No. I'm not after anything. It's just . . . well, when I think 'bout how I was . . . well, I ought to be kicked."

"I can't kick you, son, or I would have already, if I'd been made that way."

"Then I'd have remembered it to the day I died—and never forgiven you," said Harvey, his chin on his doubled fists.

"Exactly. You understand?"

"I understand. The fault's with me and no one else. All the same, something's got to be done about it."

Cheyne drew a cigar from his vest pocket, bit off the end, and began to smoke.

"Now you can go on from here," said Cheyne, slowly, "costing me between six or eight thousand a year till you're a voter. Well, we'll call you a man then. You can go right on from that, living on me to the tune of forty or fifty thousand, besides what your mother will give you, with a yacht or a fancy ranch where you can pretend to raise race horses and play cards with your own crowd."

"Like Edward Tuck?" Harvey said.

"Yep, or old man McQuade's son. California's full of 'em, and here's an Eastern example while we're talking."

A shiny black yacht, with mahogany decks and pink-and-white-striped awnings, steamed up the harbor, flying the flag of some New York country club. Two young men in bathing suits were playing cards and a couple of women with red and blue umbrellas looked on and laughed noisily.

"Wouldn't care to be caught on that boat in any sort of weather," said Harvey, critically, as the yacht slowed down and prepared to dock.

"They're having what they consider a good time. I can give you that, and twice as much, Harve. Would you like that?"

"Caesar! That's no way to drop an anchor,"

said Harvey, still watching the yacht. "If I couldn't handle an anchor line better than that, I'd stay on shore . . . What if I don't?"

"Stay on shore?"

"Yacht and ranch and live off the old man, and—hide behind Mama," said Harvey, with a twinkle in his eye.

"Why, in that case, you'll come work with me, my son."

"Ten dollars a month?" Another twinkle.

"Not a cent more until you're worth it, and that won't happen for a few years. I made the mistake of starting in business too soon. I was too young."

"A thirty million dollar mistake, though, wasn't it?"

"I lost some and I gained some. I'll tell you."

Cheyne pulled his beard and smiled as he looked over the still water. Then he began to speak to Harvey, who slowly realized that his father was telling the story of his life. He talked in a low, even voice, and it was a history for which a dozen leading newspapers would have cheerfully paid many dollars. It was a story of forty years and, at the same time, the story of America's New West.

It began with an orphan boy turned loose in Texas, and went on fantastically through a hundred twists and turns of life, the scenes shifting from state after Western state, from cities that sprang up in a month, to wild adventures in wilder settlement camps that are now working towns. It covered the building of three railroads. It told of steamers, forests and mines, and of men from every imaginable country working, creating, digging and harvesting these things. It touched on opportunities of tremendous wealth that were missed by the slimmest accident of time and travel. And through the wild shifting of things, sometimes on horseback, more often on foot, now rich, now poor, in and out, and back and forth, deck hand, contractor, boarding house keeper, journalist, engineer, drummer, real estate agent, politician, deadbeat, rum seller, mine owner, speculator or cattleman, moved Harvey Cheyne Sr., alert and quiet, seeking his own fortune, and, so he said, the glory and advancement of his country.

He told of the faith that never deserted him, even when he hung on the ragged edge of despair. He explained, as though he was talking to himself, his very great courage and cleverness at all times. He described how he had outsmarted his enemies, or forgiven them, exactly as they had outsmarted or forgiven him in those wild days; how he had begged, persuaded, and bullied towns and companies to make room for the new railroads; how he had crawled around, through, or under mountains and ravines, dragging an iron railroad track behind him, and in the end, how he had sat still while wild men and sinful towns tore the last fragments of his character to shreds.

The tale held Harvey almost breathless, his eyes fixed on his father's face, as the sunset deepened and the red cigar end lit up his wrinkled cheeks and heavy eyebrows. To Harvey, it was like watching a train storm across the country in the dark. But this train could talk, and the words shook and stirred the boy to the core of his soul. At last Cheyne threw away the cigar butt, and the two sat in the dark over the lapping water.

"I've never told that to anyone before," said the father.

Harvey gasped. "It's the greatest story that ever was!" he said.

"That's what I got. Now I'm coming to what I didn't get. It won't sound like much of anything to you, but I don't want you to be as old as I am before you find out. I can handle men, of course, and I'm no fool, but—but—I can't compete with a man who has been educated! I never went to school, Harve. I've learned as I went along, and I guess it shows all over me."

"I've never seen it," said the son.

"You will, though, Harve. You will—just as soon as you're finished with college. Don't I know it? Don't I know the look on men's faces when they think of me as—as an unschooled buffoon? Sure, I can break them to little pieces—yes—but they still have something over me. Now you've got your chance. You've got to soak up all the learning you can, and you'll live with people who are doing the same thing. They'll be doing it for a few thousand dollars a year at most; but remember you'll be doing it for millions. You'll learn about the law so you can look after your own property when I'm gone, and you'll have to be as smart as the best men in the stock market. Above all, you'll have plain, common, sit-down-with-your-chin-on-your-elbows book learning. Nothing pays like that, Harve, and it's bound to pay more and more each year in our country—in business and in politics. You'll see."

"There's nothing sweet about my end of the deal," said Harvey. "Four years at college! Wish I'd chosen the yacht!"

"Never mind, my son," Cheyne insisted. "You're investing your capital where it'll bring in the best returns. Think it over, and let me know in the morning. Hurry! We'll be late for supper!"

Harvey and his father didn't tell Mrs. Cheyne about their conversation. But Mrs. Cheyne knew they had been talking about Harvey's future, and she was a little jealous. The boy she knew was gone, replaced by a clever and strangely silent youth who spoke mostly to his father.

"What have you two been up to?" she asked the next day, with a weak little smile.

"Talking—just talking, Mama. Don't worry. There's nothing mean about Harvey anymore."

He was right. The boy had come to a decision by himself. Cheyne explained (with a bit of disappointment) that railroads did not interest Harvey any more than lumber, real estate, or mining. What his soul yearned for was control of one of his father's newly purchased sailing ships. If that could be promised to him within a reasonable amount of time, Harvey promised to attend college for four or five years. During his vacations, he would be allowed full access to all details connected with the shipping line from his father's most private papers. Harvey had already asked more than two thousand questions about it.

"It's a deal," said Cheyne at last. "You'll change your mind twenty times before you leave college, o' course; but if you do a good job, I'll turn the ship over to you. How's that, Harve?"

"Nope. It's never a good idea to split up a family business. There's too much competition in the world anyway, and Disko says 'blood must stick together.' His crowd never turns their backs on him. He says that's one reason why they make so much money. I'll take over the business end of the ship. I'm good with numbers. But I don't want to own it, father. It should stay as part of your fleet. Say, the *We're Here* sails off to George's Island on Monday. They don't stay on shore for long, do they?"

"Well, we ought to be going, too, I guess. I've left my business hung up at loose ends between two oceans, and it's time to connect again. I just hate to do it, though. I haven't had a vacation like this for twenty years."

"We can't leave without seeing Disko off," said Harvey; "and Monday's Memorial Day. Let's stay for that, anyway."

"What is this memorial business? They were talking about it in town," said Cheyne weakly. He, too, was not anxious to spoil these golden days.

"Well, as far as I can make out, it's a sort of song-and-dance act. It's mostly for the sake of the summer boarders, so Disko don't think much of it. Disko's an independent man. Haven't you noticed that?"

"Well—yes, I have. Is it a town show, then?"

"I guess. They read out the names of the fellows drowned or lost at sea, and they make speeches and recite stories. Disko says the real show's in the springtime, when there aren't any summer boarders around."

"I see," said Cheyne, who understood these celebrations very well. He had seen countless numbers of them out West. "We'll stay over for Memorial Day, and set out in the afternoon."

"Guess I'll go down to Disko's and make him bring his crowd up before they sail. I'll have to stand with them, of course."

"Oh, that's it, is it," said Cheyne. "I'm only a poor summer boarder, and you're—"

"A banker—full-blooded banker," Harvey called back as he boarded a trolley, and Cheyne went on with his blissful dreams for the future.

Disko wasn't interested in the Memorial Day celebration. He had heard that a Philadelphia actress was going to take part in the exercises. "I can't stand them uppity types," said Disko. But Harvey pleaded that the glory of the day would be lost, so far as he was concerned, if the crew of the *We're Here* didn't show up. Disko finally agreed, but only to please Harvey, who clearly wanted to stand one last time with his shipmates.

Cheyne watched the trolleys hurrying into town in the hot, hazy morning. They were full of women in light summer dresses, and men in straw hats fresh from Boston. There were stacks of bicycles outside the post office; the come-and-go of busy officials greeting one another; the slow wave of colorful streamers in the heavy air; and the important man with a hose washing the brick sidewalk.

Mrs. Cheyne looked down the crooked street. Like her husband, she was also familiar with these gatherings. The fishermen began to mingle with the crowd around the town hall doors—Portuguese, Nova Scotians, French, Italians, Swedes, and Danes, and everywhere women in black, who saluted one another with heavy-hearted pride, for this was their day of great days. And there were ministers of many religions, owners of schooner fleets, bankers and marine insurance agents, captains of tug boats, boat builders, and all the mixed people of the waterfront.

They drifted along the line of seats, and one of the town officials patrolled and perspired till he shined all over with pure pride. Cheyne had met him for five minutes a few days before, and the men understood each other very well.

"Well, Mr. Cheyne, and what d'you think of our city? You have this kind of thing out West, I presume?"

"Yes, but our cities aren't as old as yours."

"That's true, of course. You ought to have been here when we celebrated our two hundred and fiftieth birthday. I tell you, Mr. Cheyne, the old city did herself credit."

"So I heard. Why doesn't this town have a first-class hotel, though?"

"Why, that's what I tell 'em all the time, Mr. Cheyne. There's big money in it, but I guess that don't affect you any. What we want is—"

Suddenly, an organ began to play.

"Our new organ," said the official proudly to Cheyne. "Cost us four thousand dollars, too. Those are some of our orphans standing up to sing. My wife taught 'em. See you again later, Mr. Cheyne. I'm wanted on the platform."

The children's voices were high, clear, and beautiful, and they quieted the last noise of those settling into their seats.

"O all ye works of the Lord, bless ye the Lord: praise him and magnify him forever!"

The women throughout the hall leaned forward to look as the children's voices filled the air. Mrs. Cheyne began to breathe quickly. She hadn't known there were so many orphans in the world, and instinctively searched for Harvey. He had found the men of the *We're Here* at the back of the audience, and was standing between Dan and Disko. Uncle Salters, who had returned the night before with Penn, greeted him suspiciously.

"Hain't your folk gone yet?" he grunted. "What are ye doin' here, young feller?"

"O ye seas and floods, bless ye the Lord: praise him, and magnify him forever!"

"Hain't he got a right to be here, same as the rest of us?" said Dan.

"Not in them clothes," Salters snarled.

"Shut your head, Salters," said Disko. "Stay right where ye are, Harve."

Then the main speaker welcomed the crowd to Gloucester. He talked about the wealth of the city, which came solely from the sea, and spoke of the price that must be paid for the yearly fishing harvest. Later, they would hear the names of those who were lost at sea—one hundred and seventeen in total. Gloucester could not brag about its prosperous mills or factories. Her sons worked for whatever money the sea offered. The most that folks ashore could accomplish was to help the widows and orphans, and after a few general remarks he took this opportunity, in the name of the city, to appeal for donations.

"I jest despise the public beggin' fer money," growled Disko. "It don't give folks a fair idea of us. Makes us seem like poor folk who can't take care of our own."

"Ef folk won't be led by conscience to help those who need it," returned Salters, "it stands to reason they hev to be shamed. You take warnin' by that, young feller. Riches endureth but for a moment, ef you waste 'em solely on luxuries . . ."

"But to lose everything, everything," said Penn. "What can you do then?" His watery blue eyes stared up and down as if looking for something to steady them. "I once read—in a book, I think—of a boat where everyone was run down—except someone—and he said to me—"

"Hush!" said Salters, cutting in. "You should read a little less an' take more interest in your dinner, Penn."

Harvey, who was jammed among the fishermen, felt a creepy, crawly, tingling thrill that began in the back of his neck and ended at his boots. He was cold, too, even though it was a stifling hot day.

"That the actress from Philadelphia?" said Disko Troop, scowling at the platform. "I can't stand them uppity types."

The woman delivered some sort of poem about a fishing port called Brixham and a fleet of trawlers beating against a storm by night, while the women made a guiding fire at the head of the pier with everything they could find.

They took the grandma's blanket,
Who shivered and begged them go;
They took the baby's cradle,
Who could not tell them no.

"Whew!" said Dan, peering over Long Jack's shoulder. "That's great! Must ha' bin expensive, though, burnin' all that stuff."

And knew not all the while
If they were lighting a bonfire
Or only a funeral pile.

The wonderful voice captivated the audience. As she told how the drenched crews were flung ashore, living and dead, and they carried the bodies by the glare of the fires, asking, "Child, is this your father?" or "Wife, is this your man?" you could hear quiet sobbing throughout the crowd.

And when the boats of Brixham
Go out to face the sea,
Think of the love that travels
Like light upon their sails!

There was very little applause when she finished. The women were looking for their handkerchiefs, and many of the men stared at the ceiling with moist eyes.

"Hmm," said Salters, "that 'u'd cost ye a dollar to hear at any theatre—maybe two. Some folk, I presoom, can afford it. Seems downright wasteful to me. Now, how in Jerusalem did Captain Bart Edwards end up here?"

"No keepin' him away," said a man from Eastport, Maine, who was standing nearby. "He's a poet, an' he's bound to say his piece. 'Comes from down my way, too."

For five years, Captain Bart Edwards had begged for a chance to recite his very own poem on Gloucester Memorial Day. An amused and exhausted committee had at last given into his request. The simplicity and utter happiness of the old man, as he stood up in his very best Sunday clothes, won the audience over before he opened his mouth. They sat quietly through thirty-seven terrible verses that described, at great length, the loss of the schooner *Joan Hasken* off George's Island in the great storm of 1867. When he finally came to the end, they cheered with one kindly voice.

A Boston reporter slid away for a full copy of the epic poem and an interview with the author. This was the most thrilling moment for Captain Bart Edwards, ex-whaler, master-fisherman, and poet, in the seventy-third year of his life.

"Now, that's what I call fine writing," said the man from Eastport.

"Dan could do better'n that with one hand before breakfast," said Salters. "But I guess he's fairly literary—fer Maine."

"Guess Uncle Salters's goin' to die this trip. First compliment he's ever paid me," Dan snickered. "What's wrong with you, Harve? You're actin' all quiet and you look greenish. Feelin' sick?"

"Don't know what's the matter with me," Harvey replied. "Seems as if my insides were too big for my outsides. I'm all woosey and shivery."

"Bad stomach? We'll wait for the readin', an' then we'll leave, an' catch the tide."

The widows braced themselves like people about to be shot in cold blood. They knew what was coming. The summer boarder girls in pink and blue dresses stopped giggling over Captain Edwards's poem, and looked back to see why everyone was silent. The fishermen pressed forward as that town official who had talked to Cheyne stepped up on the platform and began to read the year's list of losses. His voice rang very loudly in the stillness of the hall, as he announced each name, and the sailor's country of origin:

"September 9th—Schooner *Florrie Anderson* lost, with all aboard, off George's Island.
Reuben Pitman, captain, 50, single, Gloucester.
Emil Olsen, 19, single, Denmark.
Oscar Standberg, single, 25, Sweden.
Carl Stanberg, single, 28, Gloucester.
Joseph Welsh, single, 30, Newfoundland.
Charlie Ritchie, Nova Scotia, 33, single.
September 27th—Orvin Dollard, 30, married, drowned in dory off Eastern Point."

One of the widows cried out where she sat, clasping and unclasping her hands. Mrs. Cheyne, who had been listening with wide-opened eyes, hung her head and choked. Dan's mother, a few seats to the right, quickly moved to her side. The reading continued. By the time they reached the January and February wrecks, the widows were quietly weeping.

"February 23rd—Schooner *Gilbert Hope.*
Robert Beavon went astray in dory, 29, married, native of Nova Scotia."

But his wife was in the hall. They heard a low cry, as though a little animal had been hit. She had been hoping against hope for months, because some who have gone adrift in dories have been miraculously picked up by deepsea sailing ships. Now she was sure that her husband was dead.

"April 19th—Schooner *Mamie Douglas* lost on the Banks with all aboard.
Edward Canton, 43, captain, married, Gloucester.
David Hawkins, 34, married, Nova Scotia.
G.W. Clay, 28, married, Gloucester."

And so on, and so on. Great lumps were rising in Harvey's throat, and his stomach reminded him of the day when he fell from the passenger ship.

"May 10th—Schooner *We're Here.* Otto Svendson, 20, single, lost overboard."

Once more a low, tearing cry was heard at the back of the hall. It was Otto's fiancée.

"She shouldn't ha' come. She shouldn't ha' come," said Long Jack, shaking his head in pity.

"Don't you faint, Harve," grunted Dan. Harvey heard that much, but the rest was all darkness and dizziness. Disko leaned forward and spoke to his wife, where she sat with one arm around Mrs. Cheyne.

"Harve's gone down. Better hev his mama tend to him," he whispered.

"I ca-an't! I do-don't! Oh, let me—" Mrs. Cheyne did not know what she was saying.

"You must," Mrs. Troop repeated. "Your boy's jest fainted dead away. We can git out on this side. You come right along with me, my dear. Come!"

The men of the *We're Here* moved through the crowd like bodyguards, and propped up a very white and shaken Harvey on a bench outside.

"How d'you think he could ever stand it?" she cried angrily to Cheyne, who had said nothing at all. "It was horrible—horrible! We shouldn't have come. It's wrong and wicked! It—it isn't right! Are you better, darling?"

That made Harvey very ashamed. "Oh, I'm all right, I guess," he said, struggling to his feet, with a broken giggle. "Must ha' been something I ate for breakfast."

"Coffee, perhaps," said Cheyne quietly. "We won't go back in."

"Guess it's 'bout time we git down to the pier anyways," said Disko.

Harvey announced that he never felt better in his life, but when he saw the *We're Here* at Wouverman's pier, he was hit with another overwhelming feeling—a strange mixture of pride and sorrow. Other people—mostly summer boarders—played about in rowboats or looked at the sea from the piers. But he understood things from the inside—more things than he could begin to think about. Nonetheless, he could have sat down and wept because the little schooner was going away. Mrs. Cheyne simply cried and cried every step of the way. Mrs. Troop "babied" her till Dan, who had not been "babied" since he was six, whistled aloud.

And so the old crowd dropped into the old schooner among the battered dories, while Harvey slipped the rope from the pier hook, and they slid her out into the water. Watching them, Harvey felt like the most ancient of mariners. Everyone wanted to say so much that no one said anything in particular. Harvey reminded Dan to take care of Uncle Salters's jellyfish stings and Penn's dory anchor, and Long Jack reminded Harvey to remember his lessons in seamanship. But nobody laughed at the jokes. It is hard to be funny with the ocean water widening between good friends.

"Up jib and foresail!" shouted Disko, standing at the wheel as the wind took hold of the *We're Here*. "See you later, Harve. I've come to think quite fondly of you and yer folks."

Then she glided away, and they sat down to watch her sail up the harbor. All the while, Mrs. Cheyne wept.

"Hush, my dear," said Mrs. Troop. "Crying won't ease your heart. God knows it's never done me a bit o' good." Then, after a pause: "God also knows I've had a lot to cry for."

Now it was a few years later, on the western coastline of America. A young man walked through the clammy sea fog, up a windy street that was lined with expensive houses. As he stood by a large iron gate, another young man rode up on a fine, thoroughbred horse. This is what they said:

"Hello, Dan!"

"Hello, Harve!"

"What's the news with you?"

"Well, I'm working as the captain's right-hand man. Ain't you almost through with that fancy college of yours?"

"Almost. I tell you, our new tea ship can't hold a candle to the old *We're Here*, but I'm coming into the business for good next fall."

"On my ship? The one I work on?"

"That's right. You just wait till I get my knife into you, Dan. I'm going to make the whole crew lie down and cry when I take charge."

"I'll risk it," said Dan, with a brotherly grin, as Harvey climbed down from his horse and asked whether he was coming in.

"That's why I came. But say, is the doctor around? I'll drown that crazy feller some day, just fer his one cussed prediction."

There was a low, triumphant chuckle, as the ex-cook of the *We're Here* came out of the fog to take the horse's bridle.

"Foggy as the Banks, ain't it, doctor?" said Dan.

But the mysterious cook with the second-sight did not reply till he had tapped Dan on the shoulder, and for the twentieth time, spoke the old, old prophecy in his ear.

"Master—man. Man—master," said he. "You remember, Dan Troop, what I said? On the *We're Here*?"

"Well, I won't deny it. Seems as if you were correct, doctor" said Dan. "The *We're Here*, she was a noble schooner, and fer many reasons, I owe her a heap—her and Dad."

"Me too," said Harvey Cheyne.

AFTERWORD

About the Author

Rudyard Kipling was born in Bombay, India, in 1865. He wasn't Indian though; he was British. At that time, India was a British colony, and the Kiplings were one of many British families who had moved to India in hopes of making their fortune there. They had left England when Kipling's father had been offered a job teaching at a Bombay art school.

Kipling's early childhood seems to have been a very happy one. Even those British families who did not have much money could afford servants in India. Like the main character in *Captains Courageous*, Harvey Cheyne, little Rudyard grew up being cared for by a team of servants including a nanny, a cook, and other people who helped around the house. He spent so much time with them that he learned Hindustani (the main language of India) before he learned English. Living among his Indian friends, hearing their stories, and soaking up the sounds and sights around him, he developed a deep love for India and its culture. As an adult, he would set many of his finest pieces of writing there, including his most famous novel, *The Jungle Book.*

When Kipling was five years old, his life changed dramatically. India, with its hot climate, was home to dangerous tropical diseases. Also, there were not many British-style schools in India. For these reasons, many British parents at that time sent their children back to Great Britain to be educated. This is what happened to Kipling. His parents traveled with him to England and left him there, to be cared for by paid foster parents. He was desperately unhappy about his new home, and as an adult, he wrote bitterly about this period of life in several short stories.

When he was twelve, Kipling left his foster home for a British boarding school where he was plunged into a wild, rowdy atmosphere of bullying, teasing, and practical jokes. Kipling had poor eyesight and was never much of an athlete, but he earned the other boys' respect as a talented writer, became editor of the school newspaper, and made a handful of lifelong friends.

Although Kipling would have liked to attend college, his family couldn't afford to send him, so he returned to India at the age of sixteen and started writing for a newspaper there. Covering local news taught the young journalist a great deal, and he soon became popular with readers. He began writing short stories in his spare time, many of them based on events he had witnessed as a reporter. Some of his stories were reprinted in a series of books called the Indian Railway Library, which were sold to travelers in railroad stations. Through the people who read them, Kipling's reputation began to spread across India and overseas. By the time Kipling moved back to England in 1889 and published his first novel, *The Light that Failed*, he was famous both in England and the United States.

Kipling married an American woman, Carrie Balestier, and the couple moved to Vermont. It was here that Kipling drew upon his New England surroundings to write *Captains Courageous*. It is the only novel of his to be set in America.

The book was written at a difficult time in Kipling's life. He and his wife had argued with her brother, Beatty Balestier, who lived close by in Vermont. In early May of 1896, he attacked Kipling and threatened to kill him. Kipling eventually took his brother-in-law to court, which attracted a lot of negative publicity for the famous writer. It was during this time that Kipling traveled to Boston and Gloucester. On August 31, he told a friend that his American novel was finished. The very next day, the Kiplings left for England after four years in

Vermont. The argument with his brother-in-law had driven Kipling to leave the U.S.

This was not the only tragedy to face Kipling. By this time, he and Carrie had three children: Josephine, Elsie, and John. Sadly, only Elsie survived into adulthood. Josephine died of pneumonia when she was just a little girl. When the First World War broke out, John enlisted and was killed in his first battle. He was eighteen. To add to his parents' heartbreak, he was buried somewhere in France in an unmarked grave, which his parents were never able to locate. Both the Kiplings suffered deep depression over the loss of their son.

Despite his sadness, Kipling continued to be an extremely productive author for most of his life. He won the Nobel Prize for Literature in 1907, becoming the first British winner of that award.

About the Book

Captains Courageous was written over 100 years ago, yet it endures as a captivating tale of adventure, friendship and courage. It is the story of young Harvey Cheyne, a spoiled upper-class boy whose life is changed forever when he is rescued by the colorful men of a Massachusetts fishing ship named, *We're Here*. Through vivid descriptions, engaging characters and nearly non-stop action, Kipling immerses us in life aboard the indomitable ship. The work is dangerous and full of unexpected challenges that keep us turning the page to see what will happen next. Will Harvey survive his voyage at sea? And how will this experience change him?

When we first meet Harvey, he is traveling to Europe aboard a luxury ocean liner. He is the son of Harvey Cheyne, Sr., a wealthy—and ruthless—railroad tycoon who spends most of his time away from home, building his fortune. Mrs. Cheyne has struggled to raise young Harvey alone, but his wild behavior and spoiled tantrums have worn her down. She has given up trying to discipline her son, and is now taking him to boarding school.

Harvey is in desperate need of parenting. As one character describes it, ". . . there's a heap of good in the boy if you could get at it." But for now, the good side of Harvey is obscured by his arrogance. Although he is only 15 years old, he believes he can order people around. The result, as one man describes it in the opening lines of the book, is that Harvey is "the biggest nuisance aboard." He brags, he swaggers, and, as readers, we do not like him very much.

Harvey's upper-class life takes an unexpected turn when he is suddenly washed overboard in the vast North Atlantic. Soon, Harvey finds himself on the decks of the schooner *We're Here*, which is headed to the Grand Banks for a season of cod fishing. At first, Harvey is convinced that his status as a millionaire's son will compel the captain, Disko Troop, to immediately turn the ship around. Much to his surprise, however, Disko does not believe Harvey's fantastical tales of wealth. In fact, the captain is convinced that Harvey is "confused in the head." He takes pity on the boy, and offers him a job for $10.50 a month, which is a fraction of Harvey's usual allowance. Although he has never worked a day in his life, Harvey has no other choice. He accepts Disko's offer and joins the crew of the *We're Here*.

At first, Harvey is outraged at the notion of doing such menial work as scrubbing pots and cleaning floors. But he quickly learns that the men of the ship will not indulge his tantrums. Disko, the imposing but fair-minded captain, takes a firm stand with Harvey. He expects him to work just as hard as the other men, and in the dangerous waters of the Grand Banks, laziness will not be tolerated. The crewmates must work together and look out for each other if they are to survive the treacherous North Atlantic waters.

Someone is finally standing up to Harvey and, as a result, Harvey begins to change into a responsible and humble young man. He thrives under the discipline and care of his new family. He learns how to stack the dory boats on deck, and catches his first fish. He stands watch at night, and rings the fog bell in bad weather. He begins to feel proud of himself, and even swells with pride whenever he thinks of his modest month salary. But most of all, for the first time in his life, Harvey feels like he matters. His role on the ship is important, and he strives to earn the respect of his fellow shipmates. By the time the men return to Massachusetts, it is hard to remember how spoiled Harvey once was.

Who will Harvey become when he grows up? Will he follow in his father's footsteps? Or will he follow Disko's example? Harvey Cheyne, Sr. is a powerful businessman, but he is not a very good person. He has earned his millions by destroying his enemies. He is also a terrible father who barely knows his own son. In contrast, Disko Troop has achieved success by treating his crew with fairness. He is a wonderful father, and is admired by everyone as an honest and just man.

In the end, Harvey takes the best of both men. At the conclusion of the novel, Harvey and his new best friend, Dan, have moved to California. With the help of Harvey's father, they both have promising careers aboard modern ships. There is no doubt that Harvey will be wealthy in the future. However, he has also learned about hard work, integrity and friendship, thanks to Disko's guidance and his experience on the *We're Here*.

But *Captains Courageous* isn't just about Harvey. It is also about the colorful and intriguing men of the *We're Here*. Each man on the boat has a unique life story that unfolds throughout the novel. There is Manuel, the sweet-natured sailor from Portugal who rescues Harvey from certain death; and Long Jack, the rough-and-tumble Irishman. Tom Platt is a Navy veteran who has survived many battles at sea. Who can forget the endearing story of Pennsylvania Pratt, the former minister who is still in shock from the death of his family? These characters provide us with page after page of entertainment. They make us laugh with their humorous antics, and move us with their loyalty and courage. We admire their skill as fisherman, and applaud their victory as the first schooner to return to Massachusetts with a full load of fish. *Captains Courageous* is one of the few novels to capture the unique New England fishing culture. It allows us to experience the powerful bond that forms between these hard-working men who spend months together at sea. It is a thrilling experience that most readers will never forget.

Captains Courageous is an exciting tale of adventure on the high seas. Using vivid descriptions and details, Kipling puts us on the decks of an old-world fishing schooner, and takes us on a thrilling ride through the dangerous North Atlantic. We meet a colorful cast of characters from every imaginable walk of life. The story is even more exciting because it is told through the eyes of Harvey Cheyne, a frightened young boy who must find his way in an unfamiliar world. Chances are you will be swept away by this compelling story from one of literature's great writers.

If you liked
Captains Courageous
**you might be interested in other
books in the Townsend Library.**

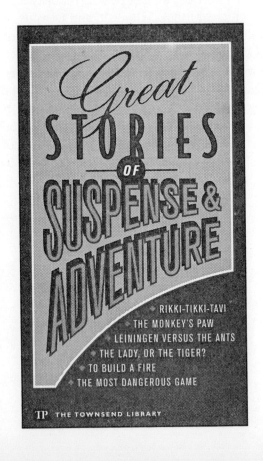

Great
STORIES
OF
SUSPENSE &
ADVENTURE

* RIKKI-TIKKI-TAVI
* THE MONKEY'S PAW
* LEININGEN VERSUS THE ANTS
* THE LADY, OR THE TIGER?
* TO BUILD A FIRE
* THE MOST DANGEROUS GAME

TP THE TOWNSEND LIBRARY

MARK TWAIN

The
Prince AND *The* Pauper

TP THE TOWNSEND LIBRARY

(continued on the following pages)

THE JUNGLE BOOK

❦

RUDYARD KIPLING

THE TOWNSEND LIBRARY   TP

JACK LONDON

The
CALL
of the
WILD

TP THE TOWNSEND LIBRARY

TARZAN
►► OF THE APES ◄◄

EDGAR RICE BURROUGHS

TP THE TOWNSEND LIBRARY

ROBERT LOUIS STEVENSON
Treasure Island
TP THE TOWNSEND LIBRARY

The Merry Adventures of
RobinHood

HOWARD PYLE

TP THE TOWNSEND LIBRARY

EDGAR RICE BURROUGHS

A
PRINCESS
OF MARS

TP THE TOWNSEND LIBRARY

Dracula

BRAM STOKER

THE TOWNSEND LIBRARY TP

For more information, visit us at
www.townsendpress.com